Speaking for the Oak

By

Stella Stafford

Is Little Wychwell really turning into Camelot? Who is Nimuë and what is the mystery at the White House? Can the villagers of Little Wychwell and Upper Storkmorton save the Boundary Oak from Developers? Finn, Flipper, Stinker, Barnabus and Elodea are all back in the tenth Little Wychwell Mystery.

This is the tenth Little Wychwell mystery.

Speaking for the Oak is

Little Wychwell Mystery Number Ten

It follows:

Did Anyone Die?

A Very Quiet Guest

All that Glisters is not Silver

Speak of the Wolf

Some People Go Both Ways

Walking Where the Willows Whisper

A Walrus in Oxford

A Cellist in the Well

Amare Valde

This is the 10th Little Wychwell Mystery. Although these books can be read standalone they are part of a series about the same family and village so reading them in order may be easier to follow.

DISCLAIMER
This is a work of fiction and the views and opinions of my characters do not represent my own views and opinions. The characters are not based on any real people, either alive or dead.

The people, research projects, most of the places and everything else in this book do not exist and have never existed.

Any resemblance between any of the people or the invented places or invented research projects or invented jobs in security like those of Finn and Flipper or invented anything else in this book and real places, research projects, real people, real jobs or real anything else is wholly accidental.

Dedicated with much love to all the trees, plants and greenfields that keep us and the whole Planet alive and who need us to speak for them

Chapter One

Finn glided silently into the Old Vicarage kitchen. Elodea was sitting on a hard kitchen chair with her head on the table, fast asleep. She looked very peaceful even if more care worn than the last time he had seen her, he could see new frown lines on her forehead.

"Bother!" Finn said to himself, "I *overdid* the silent entry, I thought she would be baking not sleeping! Now how to wake her up without her shrieking?"

He leant downwards, put his arm gently round her shoulders and planted a kiss on her forehead.

She smiled and opened her eyes. Then she focused on his face.

"*Finn*! I thought you were *Barnabus*! How lovely to see you!" she said, remembering after her first two words that Finn should not be there and lowering her voice to a whisper.

"Hello Elodea!" said Finn, "Sorry for the kiss but you looked so much like my own Mother!"

"And I thought *you* were Barnabus!" Elodea said, adding hastily "I didn't mind" just in case he thought she was offended. She continued, "What is life without friendly hugs and kisses? It was so awful in the pandemic, not being allowed to hug and kiss people!"

Elodea gave Finn a beaming smile and then looked sterner "Finn you *really shouldn't be here*!" she said, "You know how John feels about *you and Flipper*! He is still working from home most of the time so he could appear in the kitchen at any moment!"

"It's OK!" said Finn, putting the kettle on, getting some mugs out and preparing to make them both a cup of coffee, "He's in an online meeting for *hours*!"

"Oh Finn!" said Elodea, rather exasperated, "I suppose you checked his online schedule before you called round! What happens if John's meeting finishes *early*?"

"No chance!" said Finn, confidently "One of the participants is known for long boring speeches and wandering off the point at every opportunity. I would say noon at the *very* earliest. They were all droning on like fury when I had a quick look in through his window on the way past!"

"*Finn!*" said Elodea, "What if John had *seen* you? He has a new security system on the house, which he only put in *because* of *you and Flipper*, and it will *definitely* have picked you up! He'll be down any *second!*"

"No chance" said Finn again, "Very clever system though, I thought he must have designed it himself, really *very* impressive! But, Elodea, I can *assure* you that there is no such thing as a security system that is *Finn* proof! *Arare litus!*[1]"

Elodea sighed again. Finn and Flipper were *lovely* people and she loved having them visit, but she wished they would not just pop up like this. First because they were *never* there for a good and harmless reason and second because she knew that John would be *so* disappointed if he knew his anti-operative security system had not worked. Then Elodea brightened up as, after all, what John did not know would not worry him.

"How are *the family*?" asked Finn, handing her a mug of coffee and hunting through the cake tins, "Ah, *my favourite*, your coffee sponge!"

"Feel free! I'll have a slice too, please!" said Elodea, rejecting the idea of trying to explain the principles of why he should not call in when unwanted as, after all, she enjoyed his visits herself.

Elodea paused momentarily for thought so she could review what her scattered children and grandchildren were doing currently and then continued, "The *family*. Where to even start? Well, as you will know, Angel gave up working at the Frog in Pond to look after the children after the last episode you and Flipper were involved with here. You made Angel worry that the Old Vicarage was not a healthy place for her children due to it being nearly being blown up by a crashing aircraft[2]. Plus she also worried about getting a new and exotic branch of Covid during the Pandemic because of all the International Visitors at the Frog in Pond and

---

[1] Erasmus in Adagia, 'To plough the seashore' or 'wasted effort'
[2] Little Wychwell 9 – Amare Valde

then giving it to everyone else and someone in the family dying from it. So she gave up working after all these years and, rather to everyone's surprise, she took to *not working* like a duck to water, as the saying goes. She is really enjoying village life and activities with the other Mothers. But she is often exhausted with the Twins, even with them in Nursery School and nearly into the Reception Class now, let alone being run ragged by the two girls, who are still *positively wild*. I have the Twins here quite often just to give Angel and Barnabus a little break from them. Even though they are *my own* grandchildren and I absolutely *adore* them both, I have to tell you, Finn, that Augustus and Julius can be what is politely called *Challenging* to look after!"

"Julius and Augustus?" asked Finn, "Angel and Buffy haven't had any *more* children have they?"

"No, no, that's *the Twins*! But I am trying to call them by their correct names instead of 'The Twins'. It is so bad for them to keep being referred to as if they were one object, they need to be encouraged to develop individual personalities and become less dependent on each other. But it's so much easier to just label them as The Twins especially as they seem so interlocked. It's pure laziness on all our parts!" said Elodea.

"Quite! Absolutely!" said Finn, who had stopped listening once he had established that Julius and Augustus were 'The Twins' and that his briefing had not forgotten to mention two new arrivals. Finn continued *"Angel* not likely to *call in?"*

"No, no, she has gone to the gym for her keep fit class this morning and she and the other girls always have lunch in the café there afterwards!" said Elodea, then to avoid sexism added, "And any men in the class, of course, they *all* have lunch in the café there afterwards. Not that I think there are any men in the class currently."

'Angel's activities are exactly as I predicted!' thought Finn, 'Splendid!'

"Buffy getting on OK?" asked Finn, even though he knew he was.

"A lot less tired now Angel is taking on more of the child care but he has been promoted and works all hours instead. But surely you already knew that? Haven't you popped in and seen him lately?" asked Elodea.

"No, not really seen him since I last saw you, you know, I've, er, you know, I've been *busy too*!" said Finn, "give him my regards if you see him!"

"Yes, of course I will!" said Elodea, while wondering whether what Finn said about not seeing Barnabus was true.

"So, Barnabus is not so tired now and he has more spare time?" mused Finn, almost to himself.

"No, Finn, whatever you are doing here currently, Barnabus is *not* going to get involved with *any* of your schemes!" said Elodea, firmly, "Not only does Angel worry about whether it is safe for you and Flipper to be in the same place as *her* children but I worry about that with *my* children as well!"

"What?" said Finn, "Buffy's *never* come to any harm from anything to do with either of us yet!"

Finn looked at Elodea's face, she did not look pleased, in fact she looked as if she was about to explode and remind him of several previous episodes that had involved himself and Flipper. So Finn added hastily, to distract her, "May I say what a beautiful *dress* you are wearing!" and slightly spoiled the effect by adding, "Or, er, *top* perhaps? *Blouse*?"

"No, no" answered Elodea, "It is a dress!"

She extricated her legs from under the table, stood up and twirled around.

"Wow!" said Finn as even he was momentarily gob smacked by the sight of a full length apricot silk and old lace ball gown whirling around with Elodea, "Are you, er, going out somewhere shortly?"

"No, no" said Elodea again, "It's just what I'm wearing today!"

"Absolutely! Entirely up to you! Charming!" said Finn, "You must have a chat with Flipper sometime, very fashion conscious, Flipper is, you should see his running gear! He would love *that* style!"

"Oh, no, it's not *fashion*, Finn, it's *a ball gown from when I was at college*!" said Elodea.

She smiled at him and left a pause for about thirty seconds before taking pity on him.

"You see, Finn, last time that John took some of his annual leave he said that since we were not booking holidays away at present due to the risk of Covid or another sudden lockdown or whatever else might happen, he intended for us to spend *some useful time decluttering!*" Elodea said.

"*Decluttering*?" asked Finn, trying not to look too pointedly around the kitchen worksurfaces and shelves which were covered with the usual piles of assorted and inexplicable things, most of which had migrated there years or even decades ago.

"*Yes, decluttering! So*, I started on my wardrobe!" replied Elodea

"Ah!" replied Finn, still not seeing it at all.

"I looked at all these gorgeous clothes that live in my wardrobe but that I never wear and John said that it was obvious I would *never ever* wear them again and so they needed to *go*. So I thought about it and realised that if I took them to a charity shop they would probably not sell and then they would finish up in a textile disposal scheme and be shredded or sent abroad and piled up in a desert/ Even if someone did buy them they might chop them all up and recycle them into tea towels or something. But John is *right*, it is *wasteful* to buy new clothes when you *have* clothes already and we must preserve the Planet and if I just leave them in the wardrobe the children will throw them all away when I die, although I hope that event is many years ahead!" said Elodea.

"Ah!" said Finn again.

"*Thus*" said Elodea, "I realised it would be *far more sensible* if I threw out all my old worn-out everyday clothes and put *them* in the textile recycling scheme and then wear these really wonderful nearly completely unused clothes *myself*! So I do. I wear them to walk Grandson of Babe and to do the housework and cook and *everything*. They are so well made and comfortable and so beautifully *swishy* that I am absolutely having an *amazing time*!"

The huge pile of grey fur in the corner which had opened one eye and languidly wagged a tail when Finn appeared and then returned to slumbering now suddenly sat bolt upright at the words "walk Grandson of Babe". He looked round expectantly, saw no sign of his lead in Elodea's hand and collapsed back into an inanimate furry rug.

"Super idea! Must say it looks *fabulous*!" said Finn, who was having to resist a very unwise impulse to say, "And what does John think of this plan?"

Finn managed the alternative phrase "And did John declutter anything too?"

"Oh yes, John has *so* much energy when he is not working! He decluttered *the whole drawing room* in that fortnight!" replied Elodea.

"The Drawing Room?" asked Finn, "The one with all the tottering piles of books and dust and spiders and collapsing settees?"

"You make it sound *much worse* that it was!" said Elodea, huffily, "It's a shame you didn't come to see John and not me! He would have *agreed* with you! I liked it just as it was, it was *so comfortable* and you never had to worry about the grandchildren or Grandson of Babe *wrecking* it."

"Very good point!" replied Finn, just in time to prevent her becoming apoplectic, "Shall I go and have a quick look at the new version?"

"Only if you are *very quiet*" said Elodea, "If John finds out you are here I do not answer for the consequences!"

Finn melted out of the kitchen without a sound and then rematerialized as though he had been there all the time.

"Astonishing!" Finn said, "I would not have recognised it as the same room."

"It is quite a change isn't it?" said Elodea, "I expect I will get *used* to it in time."

"Change is the right word!" said Finn.

"The *red leather*, the *parquet floor*, the *orderly shelves!*" said Elodea, and sighed, "It's not like home at all! Of course John had to throw a lot of the books away because when he moved them they had insect or mice damage or the pages fell out when you picked them up. Then there were all the ones we did not even know we had and would definitely never read again or ever miss. He took those to the Charity Shops. What we have left on the shelves is those that we are more likely to read again. I'm afraid I left it all to him because it was so sad to have to throw old friends away even if they were worn out and unreadable. *In omnibus requiem quaesivi, et nusquam inveni nisi in angulo cum libro[3]!*"

Elodea sighed.

Then Elodea continued "So, as you can imagine, I am not sure that John's idea of 'will never read again' actually matched mine. I have not dared check exactly what has gone. But, Finn, among all the other worn out and 'will never be read agains's...he definitely got rid of almost all of Priscilla's books because he told me he had done so at dinner that evening! Even though they were not worn out at all but because only I have ever read them and then only once and will never re-read them. This is perfectly true as much as I love Priscilla because she is my *friend* even I wouldn't struggle through her books myself if she was not likely to give me a viva voce examination on their contents the next time we meet. As you know they are very academic, almost completely incomprehensible and you have to also be very into the latest feminist stance to follow them at all. But she works *so hard* on them and it is very good for me to read something quite so erudite and well written from time to time. I enjoy the pure lyricism of the writing even if I reading without much comprehension. John just said "Autre temps autre moeurs" when I pointed out that this would very much distress Priscilla if she ever found out. I suppose he is right, we must move *forwards* and not backwards and everything seems to have changed so much since Covid first appeared. Don't you think? Time seems shorter and more precious! But I still hope that Priscilla never checks these shelves or keep her in the kitchen and dining room only or something! She is bound to read all the book spines

---

[3] I have looked for peace everywhere but only found it in a corner with a book – Thomas a Kempis

on the shelves if she ever gets into the Drawing Room. I know! I will have to pretend her books are so precious I keep them somewhere else, like the bedroom or something, and then hope she doesn't ask to *see* any of them."

Elodea sighed again but before Finn could speak she resumed her monologue, "The furniture isn't *new*, John got it all from an auction. Not many people want furniture that big nowadays and because it's so out of fashion John got it for almost nothing."

"But you don't *like* the new room?" asked Finn.

"No, because it's just *not my room* anymore! I feel like my room has been *stolen*! The sofas *look* wonderful but they are hard *and* cold *and* uncomfortable! That's why I fell asleep *here*! I used to have such lovely naps in the drawing room before! But I must not be *laudator temporis acti*[4]" wailed Elodea.

"And the parquet floor? Did John lay it himself?" asked Finn.

"Oh no, that turned out to be there already, *underneath* the carpets. We had *never* seen it before. We bought all the downstairs furnishings *with* the house however many years ago *that* was!" said Elodea.

"Pre me?" asked Finn, thinking that explained how high the dust had piled up in the room before John had decluttered it, the dust must have been settling gently there for many years.

"Yes, *definitely*!" replied Elodea, "It was before you because it was also before Barnabus was born, but not very much before."

Finn took a swig of coffee and a bite of cake and moved on to a new topic.

"Delicious! How is Priscilla?" asked Finn.

"Fine as far as I know" replied Elodea, "She is currently visiting and studying Ancient Roman sites in Croatia while Charles does a geological study in the Croatian mountains. That way they can pretend to be away together while never meeting. I will never ever understand their relationship but it makes them both happy so what does it matter? As you

---

[4] Horace Ars poetica – a praiser of past times

get older, Finn, you will find these variations in relationships seem less and less important *provided people are happy!*"

Elodea smiled at Finn and then hoped he didn't think she was referring to his lifestyle too.

Finn, who had just had that very suspicion, changed the subject before Elodea asked him how Fiona was or who he was going out with now, "*And* Tony, sorry I mean *Antholian*, and Flic and, er, the *baby,* how are they all?"

"*Samaya!*" said Elodea, "Tony and Flic's daughter is called *Samaya*! Not a baby anymore either! Also Tony has given up Antholian again and gone back to Tony because it was so hard for all the other tree protestors to remember what he was called and he doesn't like being called Anthony by mistake. I expect you heard that the Frog in Pond went bankrupt due to Covid lockdowns and people not going back to hospitality and everything? This was after Angel left, it wasn't her fault. But did you *also* hear that *Flic's paren*ts have *bought* it because they liked staying there so much? They loved the very brilliant Chef and they didn't want him to lose his job and they didn't want the Frog in Pond to become a housing estate as that would be no use for them to stay in when they visit Flic and Samaya? So *having bought it* then they put *Flic* in as *the Manager*. She had no prior experience in that type of work but she is *very* good at it especially as many of the clients are either her relatives or old friends or connected to them in some way so networking is easy for her. She earns a hefty salary too, not that I think that the money genuinely comes from the Frog in Pond because hospitality is still not operating well so I expect her salary is really paid by her parents who must also be subsidizing the entire establishment. Naturally her parents can afford it, it's just small change for them. The important thing is that Tony *thinks* Flic is earning the money so he is OK with keeping it and the three of them have enough money to survive on and a bit to spare. So Tony is freed up from attempting to get a job and has become a full time Voluntary Environmental Activist and Protestor. I am sure you already know that too. Flic and Tony and Samaya are still living in the Attics here as I don't think Tony could possibly cope with *living* in the Frog in Pond or letting Flic's parents buy them a house. Flic is at the Frog in Pond in the daytime and sometimes in the evenings if there is a big reception or whatever so I am fortunate enough to get to look after Samaya a *lot* of the time and she is *such* a sweet child! Samaya is in the Frog in Pond Nursery *right now*, but she'll be back here with Flic later today!"

"And *Tony*?" asked Finn.

"*I'm sure you already know where Tony is!*" said Elodea, sounding cross.

"Admittedly I *do*. It's a shame he got *remanded* in custody just for resisting arrest" said Finn.

"A *shame*! It's an *absolute outrage*! That tree is a *vital* part of all our futures! They have *no right* to cut a huge mature oak tree down! Don't they want a Living Planet in future?" replied Elodea, her voice shooting up the scale and finishing on the C two octaves above middle C.

Finn winced at the impact on his ears.

"I know, I *know*, I know" he said in a soothing way, patting her on the back, "but I can't really asy anything about it as Official Viewpoints Must be Respected in my work!" said Finn, hoping that was enough to calm Elodea back down and wondering whether he should pick up the nearby tray ready to use it as a shield in case she started throwing things *at him*. She had got her cake plate in her hand and she looked very much as if she was either going to smash it on the floor or throw it at him.

Elodea took several deep breaths and put her cake plate back down on the table.

Then Elodea smiled at Finn, very sweetly, and said "*You* can't *do* something about it can you? Work guidelines are made to be *broken*! Tony is *coping* but it's very hard for him not to be able to go for runs and things like that although naturally he can still meditate and he is very self-sufficient. There are ten of the protestors in the same wing so they do support each other too."

"I'm genuinely sorry but sadly I'm not personally important enough to be able to get him released and even if I was it's an incident from an entirely different area to our department and not something anyone in our department could influence!" said Finn.

"Are you sure?" asked Elodea, "*Nothing at all* you can do? *Exceptio firmat regulam in casibus non exceptis*[5]"

Finn paused and thought for a couple of seconds, then a smile crossed his face, "There are a few things I *could* do. I *could* get him out illegally but you will see that if I did that it would make many more problems for *Tony's* future. It would be pretty trivial to achieve it though and no one would *ever* trace it to me!" said Finn.

"Very kind of you to offer, but *no thank you!*" replied Elodea, "I don't really want Tony permanently on the run as a fugitive from the law."

But the taut atmosphere between them had cleared and they smiled at each other again. There was a longer pause while they both engaged enthusiastically with their coffee and cake.

"So, why *are* you here?" asked Elodea, resuming conversation, "Not, not *Adam* again...please tell me he isn't back! I don't want to have to murder him *twice!*[6]"

"*Not* that you murdered him *before!*" corrected Finn "It would be the *first* time!"

"I know, Flipper came round about six months ago and told me. He thought I might be worrying about having killed him. I don't know why he suddenly thought that I might be worrying after all this time! But he was quite right, I always had it *lingering* at the back of my mind, you know, being a *murderer*. I was *so glad* to hear Adam was still alive!" said Elodea, "But Adam's *not* back in the UK? I don't think John could take the stress of him reappearing again!"

"No, no" soothed Finn, with his fingers crossed under the table, "He's, erm, under constant surveillance, you see we know *who* he is now and we know *where* he is, however well he disguises himself" he coughed and then continued, "I believe he's in, er, yes, I believe it's *Dubai* currently!"

---

[5] Literally this is "The exception confirms the rule in cases which are not excepted" but Elodea is using it for her own purposes in a commonly mistranslated way which is "It is the exception that proves the rule"

[6] The references to Adam, Elodeus and Caroline are all in Amare Valde, Little Wychwell 9

As Finn said to himself, that was not really a serious lie as living in an ex pats enclave in Dubai would be much the same as being *dead* as far as Finn was concerned. So he did not feel guilty. It was also true that they did know *who* Adam was and even *where* he was, *approximately*, even if not knowing which afterlife Adam might be in now. 'In fact I am an *entirely truthful person*!' he thought to himself.

"And Elodeus? Is he still hovering around here?" asked Finn.

"No, no, we haven't seen him *nearly* so much now he doesn't have a girlfriend whose parents live in Oxford" said Elodea, and laughed, "Caroline's Mother transferred her lectureship to Cambridge and her Father lives in College in Oxford in the week and goes to Cambridge at weekends so his girlfriend lives in the Other Place now. But Elodeus is going to take start studying for a D Phil at Cambridge next year and so is Caroline so they will be back together again! Oh no, a PhD not a D Phil! Not like Oxford, I forgot!"

"Ah!" said Finn, hoping that was an appropriate response since he had dozed off near the start of this speech.

"And Elizabeth is a Consultant now, as you probably know, and Paris is out of the Army since they inherited Belinda's Family Estate. This means he is finally tied down which he must *hate*. But he is loving the Grouse Shooting!" She sighed, "I would not enjoy that at all! We haven't been to visit them there yet because of Covid but I expect we will get there soon. I hope Paris and Belinda do not invite us for a Shoot though, neither of us shoot things and we would probably be terrible at it even if we wanted to do so!"

"Haven't seen Paris for years" said Finn, "Last time I saw him was a few years ago when we were both in Ne-"

He stopped abruptly.

"*Years* of this job and then I do that! Elodea gossiping away does something to your brain!" Finn said to himself, very angrily.

"Ne-*pal*?" finished Elodea, "So Paris went to Nepal quite *recently*? He doesn't often tell me where he is and with mobile phones you haven't the faintest idea, even if he should remember to phone me! Do you think he saw Tony and Flic while he was there? No, I am being very silly, Nepal is a huge place, not likely to even be in the same area!"

"No, Paris *definitely* didn't meet them! Not at all! He didn't see them at all!" said Finn, rather too firmly.

"It's a very big place. It would have been more surprising if they had met up I suppose! You know Samaya looks *just* like a female version of Paris at the same age, even as she gets older the resemblance is striking! Not really surprising as Paris is her Uncle and Paris looks like a male version of me and so she looks like me! She may look more like Flic when she gets older. Children change so fast as they grow!" said Elodea.

"Well, you know, *genetics are odd*" said Finn but then suddenly choked on his cake.

"Sorry" he said when he finished. He then added a completely untrue explanation "I've had Covid three times now! Sometimes I still cough!"

"*Three times*?" asked Elodea, "Did you have your vaccinations?"

"Oh yes, *definitely*, have had at least four vaccinations, or is it five or even six now?" said Finn, "Work, you know, they *insist*! Doesn't seem to do much tbh!"

"I do hope you fully recover soon!" said Elodea, "That was a very nasty coughing attack! I think I've given you a brief resume of most of the family now. *So,* your turn to tell me! Why *did* you decide to pop in again after all this time?" asked Elodea, "Not that I don't *love* seeing you Finn" she added, in case his feelings were hurt, "You *know* I do!"

"Purely *a social call*" Finn answered, "Flip's away somewhere or other and Barnabus is always busy these days and Walls is at a workshop in Harvard and Yvette without Walls[7] is definitely not suitable for a social call, I don't want a long lecture on my unavoidable complete lack of ideological soundness due to me being gender male, both assigned at birth and

---

[7] A Walrus in Oxford

current! Consequently I was just at a bit of a loose end today and I thought of *you*!"

"I suppose you expect me to *believe* that?" asked Elodea, sceptically.

"*Absolutely I do*!" answered Finn using his most charming and persuasive smile on her, "How's *Stinker*?" he continued.

"Don't you already know?" asked Elodea.

"I don't know *everything*!" Finn replied, "Plus Stinker's online presence is remarkably absent for someone our age! He even uses cash for nearly every transaction. I have no idea how he achieves that, it must be close to impossible!"

"He doesn't trust online communications or shopping" said Elodea, "For *some* reason he thinks people might be *surveilling* them, you know people who *work for the Government* might be *spying* on him!"

"How *odd*! What a vivid imagination he has! But a bit paranoid don't you think?" said Finn, maintaining a completely straight face, "So, he *has* got the Wyching Well re-open and running properly after all the lockdowns and Covid restrictions and whatever?"

"Oh yes, the Wyching Well is going *very* well. Rather a lot of pubs took lockdown loans or whatever they were called and are in terrible trouble financially now because they can't afford to repay them. So they are closing all over the place because they have these big loans and customers have still not returned to hospitality at all enthusiastically post Pandemic. But Stinker owns the Wyching Well outright and he didn't take a loan so he only has to make enough to cover costs and feed himself and things like that. The Wyching Well is so tiny that the overheads are small and Stinker isn't greedy for material things. He is very happy pottering around there and composing and playing his cello. He is very thankful all the Covid regulations are gone though. I thought he might have a nervous breakdown when he was having to forcibly apply all the rigorous Covid rules when he reopened but he's very happy again now! Running the Wyching Well fits in so well with his *musical* activities" He is *remarkably* talented you know and getting better and better known in the Classical Music sphere!" Elodea replied, "He's also an accepted part of the village now, they have gone from thinking he's a rather odd stranger in their midst to being very proud to have a real-life composer as the Pub Landlord! Did you hear it when they played the Pie Jesu from his Requiem for Therese[8] on Radio 3 the other day? I was *so* excited! That piece always makes me cry, it's *so* beautiful and *so* sad!" replied Elodea.

"I think I must have missed that. I must look it up on iplayer" said Finn, not meaning to do so at all but sounding convincing, "Erm, was Therese his *partner* or a *relative*?"

"Neither! Although I suppose in the sense that we are all related if we trace our Family Trees far enough back and wander up enough branches. So perhaps she could be a relative of *some* sort" replied Elodea.

"Good, it's not necessary to offer condolences if I see him then?" said Finn.

"No! Although he has become quite *fond* of her even if in a very abstract way" replied Elodea, obliquely.

"So, erm, who *was* she?" asked Finn, "Assuming she is actually *dead*?"

"*Very dead*. She was a Lady of Upper Storkmorton Manor in *medieval* times" replied Elodea.

"*Ah!*" said Finn, not seeing at all.

"But Stinker thinks he has met her. He thinks he saw her one night when he was out on a long cycle ride during lockdown.[9]" continued Elodea.

"*Ah!*" said Finn again, thinking that explained the strange sentence on the notes about Stinker that he had received that read '*May be delusional, see notes on Youtube for his Requiem Mass for Therese, but there is no indication that he has other than entirely harmless delusions.*' 'I must look up Stinker's Requiem Mass on Youtube *after all*!' Finn told himself.

"But" continued Elodea, "Barnabus had been *very naughty* and taken poor Stinker for *far too long* a cycle ride and made him pedal too hard and travel far too fast so I am of the opinion that Stinker's vision of Therese

---

[8] Amare Valde – Little Wychwell 9
[9] Amarc Valde Little Wychwell 9

may have been brought on by Oxygen Deprivation and Physical Exhaustion."

Elodea then spoilt this rational explanation by adding "Although we do have 'other people' in this house, you know, what most people would call 'ghosts'. They are not at all creepy. I see them myself occasionally but you can often hear them around the place, even John hears them sometimes."

"*Ah*" said Finn, in a non-committal way, wondering if staying in Little Wychwell might make him delusional himself and how long it took for this problem to develop, especially since he had been previously exposed to this danger[10], "So... do you think Stinker might be a *bit* short of money because of all the lockdowns and everything, even now the Covid regs *are* all off?"

"Hard to say" replied Elodea, "As I said, Stinker isn't very attached to money! Provided the takings cover his costs he is quite happy living on past their sell by date crisps and soft drinks so he doesn't have very many expenses. He's a bit like Tony for detachment from real life, but they are both also completely different! Stinker is as he is, whereas with Tony any eccentricities are due to applying his Principles over rigorously to his Life!"

"I might pop round and see Stinker next! I haven't seen him for ages! Splendid idea! Now that I've had that idea to fill in the rest of my day I'll stop bothering you and trot off!" said Finn.

"You aren't bothering me *at all* but John *will* be down very shortly!" said Elodea and then had a sudden thought, "Finn!" she said, with a flash of insight and deduction, "You are not thinking of *moving in with Stinker!*"

"There's an idea!" said Finn, exercising his best smile on her again, "Stinker might enjoy the extra income from a lodger, don't you think?" Then he relented and continued, "OK, I'll admit that your little set of villages do seem to attract problem people! Once you get one International Criminal moving in then the rest all copy! *Don't repeat that!* Not even to John or Barnabus!"

---

[10] Cellist in the Well, Little Wychwell 8

"I think Barnabus is going to notice you are here even if John doesn't and I expect Barnabus will be as suspicious about your motives as I am. But there is hardly any space upstairs in the Wyching Well and I don't see how he will accommodate you and……There isn't any *danger* is there? Stinker will be *safe*?" asked Elodea, "You aren't going to get Barnabus involved *again* are you?"

"No, no, no!" said Finn, soothingly, "No! It's almost impossible to even get hold of Barnabus, what with all the children and Angel not working nights any more. Haven't seen him for *ages* and *ages*! He wouldn't have *time* to get involved!"

"Just remember *the children* are all very precious! *Everyone* is very precious! *Everyone*!" said Elodea, feeling rising panic at the thought that anything else in the area might blow up if Finn and Flipper were hanging around again, aeroplanes, houses, anything!

"Don't worry!" said Finn, crossing his fingers under the table again, "No danger to *anyone* at all, including *me*! Well, I'd better hop off, John's meeting is due to end any millisecond! See you around!"

Elodea groaned, "Finn you know I love you and Flipper but you both upset John so much! You know his work is really important! He is the only person in the country who can do what he does and if he gets cross it impinges on his work and…."

"He'll be OK" said Finn, backing towards the outside door, "He'll *never* know I've been here! He doesn't *go* to the Wyching Well *does he*?"

Elodea turned to glare fiercely at Finn before she replied but Finn had already vanished from the room. She could hear John coming downstairs so she could not rush outside to catch Finn.

"Finn does like to cut it fine!" Elodea said to herself, tutting, "John only just missed bumping into him! Did Finn know exactly when John's meeting had finished? I suppose he did! I hope Finn hasn't stuck secret hidden cameras around the house again. I don't see how he could have done that while I was looking at him but then I didn't see how he and Flipper managed it last time either! *Oh no*! What a mistake I just made! I let him go and look at the Drawing Room on his own! He could have been putting monitors all over the place! But that seemed so *genuine*!"

Elodea hastily piled the used plates and mugs out of sight in the sink and put the kettle back on for herself and John. When it came to cake and coffee Elodea was always prepared to double her intake.

Chapter Two

Finn, up a tree, leaning his back on the huge supportive trunk, his legs stretched along a very thick branch, the birds singing, insects crawling around the trunk and over the branches and down his neck.

Finn, keeping still, could not swat them. He wriggled very slightly and rubbed his neck against the branch in an attempt to dislodge them. This did not work. He looked at the view to distract himself, a wonderful vision of the English countryside, topped with a bright blue sky. Almost perfect, he thought, except for a tragic lack of mountains in the vicinity of Little Wychwell which he felt would have made a beautiful backdrop. The insects continued their exploration of the inside of his clothes, occasionally stopping for a quick restorative snack of Finn-blood.

Despite the disadvantages Finn thought that it was good to get off high tech methods and back to basics. Due to the opposing side having such high tech detectors and interceptors themselves now it had been necessary to return to straightforward good old fashioned surveillance for many cases. Low tech hard to detect solutions like floating a balloon with an attached camera up from the other side of the hedge or even using a cardboard periscope or drilling a little hole in a fence or sitting up a tree in order to observe the situation were now cutting edge forefront methods again. So for this project Finn had no IT communications equipment in Little Wychwell and no connection to headquarters. Finn had, as he termed it, 'returned to The Stone Age'. For his trip up the tree he was only carrying a small camera hidden in his clothes which was detached from any network. He did not miss the constant interventions from Headquarters in his ear. This type of excursion was, he said to himself, so peaceful that it was almost perfect, provided that nothing went amiss.

Finn had climbed up the tree before it dawn and he had made himself very comfortable, anti-reflective surface flask of coffee in one pocket, biscuits in another pocket.

"This is the life!" he said to himself, "No nagging voices in my ear, fresh air, beautiful view, no one can bother me, no one can see me, no one knows I am here! Except the creepy crawlies!"

Below in the street he could see Jake Thacker and Robin Allfellow going past, one with a stick, the other with a wheeled zimmer frame.

'On their way to the Wyching Well I suppose' Finn thought, 'Wouldn't they be surprised to know they were being watched from up here! For I am invisible to them, merged into the branches like a huge pheasant, perfect!'

Far below Robin asked Jake "Is that the young man who's staying with Stinker sitting up the big oak? My eyes aren't what they were!"

"Poacher's eyes don't get old!" replied Jake, "You can see what you need to see. It *must* be him. Wouldn't be likely to be anyone from the *village* sitting up a tree at this hour of the day!"

"I wonder what he is doing of climbing up that oak" said Robin, "Isn't he the one who was writing a novel when he was staying at the Old Vicarage before?"

"That's him!" said Jake, "Maybe he's looking for his next plot up there!"

They both laughed.

"It's a shame he's up there and I that I haven't got my air rifle" Jake continued "There's a couple of fat pigeons on that low branch what would be just the ticket for a pigeon pie for tonight."

"Ah well, you can't have everything" said Robin, "It is what it is!"

They continued onwards for their pints.

High up in the branches, quite sure he was completely hidden, Finn was looking at the White House whose boundary fence was just beside his tree. It was an elegant three storey 1920s white villa with a tennis court and formal gardens, nothing overstated, the perfect size for an aspiring upper middle class family of that era, plenty of room for all the children and space for the 'live in' servants on the top floor. It had originally had stables and a carriage shed to one side, but these were now all used as garages. It looked charming and Finn found himself musing that if he himself ever settled down and had a house and a family he would like to have one just like that. Then Finn laughed, 'Flipper would think that idea was so funny he would fall over in the middle of his headstand if I told him!' he said to himself. Finn continued, 'I hope Flip's OK. He should be back in the country shortly. Hope they assign him on this project too. I could do with a second brain to think laterally on this.'

The house reposed in the sunlight. Nothing happened. From his perch Finn could see all the routes for entrance and egress. There were no visible movements. No-one appeared at the windows on the side facing the tree. The house seemed to be falling gently asleep.

Finn, basking in the sun himself, felt his eyelids closing. He got his flask out, moving slowly so no one's eye caught the movement from the ground, and had a mug of strong black coffee.

Meanwhile Stinker was busy mopping out the Wyching Well loos. He sighed, thinking to himself that many people probably thought being a Pub Landlord was a *fun* job whereas it was mostly *cleaning* and *following regulations*. Stinker thought he was glad to have Finn stay there for a while but he had hoped Finn might have been around to give him a bit of a hand with the chores in return for his free lodgings. But Finn had got up and vanished before Stinker himself had awoken. Stinker admitted to himself that since Finn was sleeping in a sleeping bag on a bench in the bar it was probably just as well that Finn had risen early as otherwise he would now be entirely in the way. Plus, and here Stinker gave himself a metaphorical hard slap on the wrist, Finn had gone to the Village Shop yesterday evening and filled up Stinker's fridge with a plentiful supply of food for both of them and cooked a huge fry up for dinner last night. "I am just being *ungrateful and grumpy*!" Stinker told himself, "It's not Finn's fault at all that I am feeling cross, it's because I wanted to get on with my new composition instead of doing the cleaning this morning! I am *ungrateful and grumpy and lazy*!"

Having told himself off Stinker brightened up, remembering that he could look forward to plentiful free food cooked by someone else as long as Finn remained there. At this idea Stinker whistled a happy tune as he finished mopping. Through the window he could see Jake and Robin sitting on the wall outside the Wyching Well already but as it was not yet opening time they would have to stay there for a while. Stinker got his ancient vacuum cleaner out and started moving the dust around behind the Bar.

Outside the Wyching Well Jake and Robin were watching Cyril the Squirrel running along the telephone wires towards *his* oak tree.

"There's our Cyril!" said Jake.

"Bit late today, must have lingered too long over his peanuts!" said Robin.

"Hope young wotsisname up that there tree likes squirrels!" said Jake.

"More to the point, Jake, it's to be hoped that *Cyril* likes *him*!" said Robin.

They both laughed.

Cyril paused for a moment, slid down a telegraph pole, picked up a piece of gravel and threw it at them both, powered back up the pole and continued onwards.

Cyril was the biggest squirrel in Little Wychwell. He terrorised any rivals off the local bird tables and made them wait till he had had his fill of goodies, he threw acorns and hazelnuts and bits of gravel at the local children and dogs and cats and, if he felt like it, at the adults too. Yet the villagers were fond of him. They were very proud of their gigantic and highly toned squirrel.

Finn, without any outside interferences, especially any voices in his ear checking on the situation, was now having great difficulty in staying awake, even with another cup of coffee. He was warmed by the sun and rocked by the gentle movement of the branches and he had to keep jerking his head upright as it fell forwards.

'Must be careful' he said to himself, 'This is a *big* branch but I don't want to fall off it! That's a long drop!'

Suddenly an acorn blasted into his forehead at high speed.

"What?" he said, out loud, forgetting to be cautious and rubbing his brow.

There was a loud chittering and swearing in 'squirrel' from just above him.

Then another acorn blasted towards him, Finn caught it as It ricocheted off his head and threw it back. Finn was at a disadvantage because Cyril was on the branch above him but he still clipped Cyril on the backside.

This was too much for Cyril. Totally enraged he slid rapidly down the trunk and appeared in front of Finn, swearing even more violently and showing his incisors off.

"Geroff!" hissed Finn.

He gave Cyril a shove with his foot.

Cyril sprang through the air towards Finn's head, Finn ducked hastily out of the way and Cyril hit the main trunk instead and clung there screaming for a few moments before whipping around ready for the next assault.

Fortunately for Finn at this precise moment an oil tanker drew into the drive of the White House.

The sight of an oil tanker on his patch annoyed Cyril even more than a human sitting in his favourite spot in the tree.

Cyril skidded down the trunk, sprinted along a low branch and began to throw a fusillade of acorns at the oil tanker, presumably enjoying the noise they made as they pinged off it.

Finn thought that he must remember to wear strong protective headware and thick gauntlet gloves if he visited this tree again.

"Thank goodness that tanker turned up!" he said.

He began to video the scene below him.

The oil tanker driver was hit with an acorn by Cyril as soon as he began to climb down from his cab to the ground so he climbed back in again and re-emerged with yellow hard hat on his head. Then he unwound the flexible hose and ran it up the drive of the White House. He fastened the nozzle to the oil tank and filled it up, ignoring the hail of acorns now bouncing off his hat as Cyril pursued him by running backwards and forwards along the top of the fence. The tank seemed to be almost empty judging by the time it took to refill it. The driver rewound the pipe and stowed it safely away, popped a receipt through the front door and drove his vehicle ponderously off.

'The amount of oil that must have been delivered in that length of time would not be at all odd' said Finn to himself, 'Had they not had their oil tank filled up yesterday too! Judging by his anti-squirrel headware reaction, this particular driver has visited before and it's not the same vehicle as yesterday unless it's had a respray with the name of different firm and new numberplates and it definitely isn't the same driver as the one whom I saw when I strolled past yesterday.'

Finn, pleased with the success of his photographic expedition, followed Cyril's example of how to leave a tree quickly by shinning quietly down the side of the trunk that was invisible to anyone in the road or in the White House. Simultaneously Cyril shinned up the opposite side to return to the branch that Finn had vacated to get to his favourite place for his afternoon nap. Finn hoped his departure would mollify Cyril but Cyril shot a final acorn at Finn as they passed each other, pinging it hard off Finn's forehead again.

'Maybe I should bring him some peanuts next time?' thought Finn, optimistically, 'If I could get him to work on *my* side that squirrel could be a great ally! His aim is superb! He would be more use as a deterrent than Flipper generally is!'

FInn laughed at his own joke and thought wandered along the same route as Jake and Robin to go back to the Wyching Well and get his own pint. Finn planned to be a polite and helpful guest and do a stint behind the bar tonight after he had made the dinner. He was bound to be able to pick up lots of useful information from the customers.

Accordingly that evening Stinker, with a very happy and full stomach, was free to go and compose leaving Finn in charge of the bar, 'Call me *at once* if anything goes even a bit wrong...*at once*! They are lovely people here but they can be easily upset and offended and they don't like change and I can't afford to lose any customers!' Stinker said, anxiously, "Some of them are not very bright compared to you so you have to be *very* patient and some of them have really strong local accents and they will think it's hilarious if you don't understand them and they will *all* try to pull your leg!"

Finn assured Stinker that he was a number one brilliant barman with years of extensive experience, which was not wholly a lie as he had done stints in the past as a barman during other projects. Then Finn promised that he would call him if, say, anything disastrous happened like the toilets blocking. Finn finished with "now go and enjoy a *lovely* bit of composing while I take the strain for you for once, you work too hard!" and hustled him up the stairs.

Stinker did not notice he was being hustled out as he was so looking forward to an evening of composition and cello playing that it did not occur to him that Finn might want to talk to his customers without him being there. Nor did he wonder when or where Finn had been a barman, lots of people worked on a bar while at College or if they were temporarily unemployed. He supposed Finn was still writing books, he had gone off to California to write film scripts with his girlfriend and clearly come back without her so Stinker, being a kind and thoughtful person, had not asked about his girlfriend either. What was her name? It started with an F, like Finn[11]. That was all Stinker could remember. The Covid pandemic seemed to have wiped his memory. Stinker had asked Finn if Flipper, who Stinker remembered was Finn's friend, was OK and Finn had said 'Yes' and Stinker had left it at that and not asked why Finn had nowhere to live right now and needed to stay in the Wyching Well. Finn was not surprised that Stinker did not ask. 'Good old Stinker!' Finn thought to himself, 'Vague and artistic friends who also run handy pubs in the right places are *the tops*!"

Robin and Jake were propping the bar up at one end, they kept ordering drinks from Finn using incomprehensible Little Wychwell nicknames for the drinks which he did not understand at all. So Finn had to get them to explain every time. This made them both chortle and choke on their drinks. They also told him the wrong prices and paid far less than they should have and they were altogether having a lovely time.

---

[11] Little Wychwell 8 A Cellist in the Well

Finn was surprised how busy the bar at the Wyching Well was, given the size of the place. He had expected a much easier evening but once the bar was too full a lot of people went outside into the tiny back garden or stood in the street or even brought their own folding chairs and sat in the street. Finn's plan for talking to the locals was not going as well as he had envisaged because with this number of customers he had to keep washing glasses inbetween serving drinks and snacks. Even worse just when he thought the customers might start leaving at about eleven thirty pm there were still more coming in.

At eleven forty five pm Finn called last orders and the customers gradually dwindled. By one pm, an hour after closing, there were just him and Robin and Jake left. Fortunately Stinker, playing melodiously onwards upstairs, had no idea that Finn had failed to remove all the customers soon after midnight or he would have been in a total panic.

"So" said Robin, "I've got to ask this before I go home tonight! What were you a doing of up that oak this lunchtime?"

'I might have known the *locals* would have spotted me' thought Finn, ruefully!

"Enjoying a bit of peace" Finn replied.

"A bit of peace? I bet as you didn't get much peace once Cyril turned up!" said Jake, laughing.

"Cyril?" asked Finn, drawing two pints, handing them to Robin and Jake and adding "On the house!"

"Cyril the Squirrel! Biggest squirrel in Little Wychwell and violent as they come! As you know even small squirrels will see any size birds right off the bird table and Cyril is one big beefy squirrel! Terror of the Village!" said Robin and chuckled, "Thank you kindly for the pint, what a gentleman you are! I shall be telling Stinker to get you on the bar more often!"

"Ah the *squirrel*!" said Finn, "He wasn't keen on sharing the tree! But an oil tanker at that big white house fortunately distracted him!"

"Ay! They does order a *lot* of oil!" said Jake, raising his pint glass to Finn before taking a long draught.

"They *do*?" asked Finn, achieving a convincing note of surprise in his voice.

"Oh ay! One or the other of they oil tankers seems to call in pretty much *every* morning!" said Jake, wiping his mouth.

"Why?" asked Finn, sounding suitably astonished.

"Well, this is something as what we would all like to know. Old Mr and Mrs Bulldock never used to have more than two deliveries a year. Even though Mr B had a set of classic Mercedes Benz cars which he might well have filled up illegally from his heating oil tank given they were all gallons to the mile cars. When I think of it though they sold that set of cars along with the house, not having any room for them in their new place, so maybe *that's* what the new people are doing with the oil? If they are using those classic cars for any distance that would take A Lot." said Jake.

"I don't see they could be driving those cars that far without any of us noticing them driving them about the place! Maybe they just order one gallon on every order and pay for the delivery?" suggested Robin, "Some kind of false economy measure? The radio was going on about trying to save fuel costs using false economy measures this morning, like candles are more expensive than the electric and not to say dangerous if left unattended. *All* their so-called new information was that *obvious*! Teaching their grandmothers to suck eggs as usual, those radio presenters!"

"I'll tell you another thing. The new owners of that White House are not very minded to support Village Businesses. None of the oil companies that deliver there are any the rest of us use to get oil deliveries, they all come from some distance away" said Robin, "They could be community minded and use Adrian Banks in the Old Yard, he supplies heating oil and gives very generous discounts to those who live in the village."

"Maybe they don't know Arthur Banks is there if they are new to the Village. Did he *offer* to deliver to the White House?" asked Finn.

"Certainly he did" replied Jake, "I mean who wouldn't with customers who seem to use oil like it was water? Adrian went and dropped a business card through the door first and then when nothing happened from that approach he tried again. This time he went and put a letter through the door telling them he was a local supplier and giving all his prices and what not. He even tried ringing the doorbell but there was no reply."

"So they didn't order from him then?" asked Finn.

"Not at all!" said Robin, "You would have thought they could have ordered one load at least from Adrian, the number of loads they are taking, just to keep in with the Village businesses, but no, nothing! The addresses on those tankers are nowhere near these parts! Further away than *Witney*!"

He said 'Witney' as though it was a distant foreign place.

"The new owners" said Jake, "don't really mix with the rest of us. I can't say as I have ever even seen them. I expect they've got half a dozen homes of their own and they revolve around them. Too many second or third or fourth or twenty-fifth homes being bought in Little Wychwell now. Owners appear at the weekend, expect the village to entertain them, complain about the cows, the cockerels, the tractors and the manure. They even complain about the beautiful crops growing and the cows being there, "so industrialized, an artificial landscape, it should all be rewilded!" I don't what they think they eat themselves. Then off they go again, back to the Big Smoke. No community spirit. No participation. No donations to Village Clubs or Activities. Don't even come in here! How's Stinker meant to keep going with half the village not being customers?"

Finn felt, after an evening on the bar, that Stinker seemed to have more than enough customers without any extra ones, but he nodded solemnly.

"So the people in the White House don't go out much?" he asked, casually.

"Well, this is a question we are not sure on. Sometimes you see the lights on at night, you hear music playing from inside, but none of us have ever seen anyone come out or go in. It's like it's a house of phantoms. It's rather on the edge of the village but our Close comes out opposite it. On the other hand you can't see that house from any of the houses in our Close because the way out at that end is just a narrow footpath inbetween two high walls so you can't see that house till you are clear of it. They only have one neighbour, because they are the last house in that piece of road, and that is old Terry. As deaf as a post so when he says he doesn't hear anyone come in or go you can't really pay much attention to that. But they don't bother no one, seem to be quite harmless!" replied Robin.

Finn handed them both another pint each.

"Now young man" said Robin, "While we are getting facts straight. What happened to that lovely fiancée of yourn? The one you went off to Hollywood with to write film scripts?[12]"

Robin said this in a voice that suggested Finn might have had a succession of fiancées since they had last met and thus needed further identification to know which fiancée it was.

"Ay, she was a looker and no mistake!" said Jake, reminiscently, and having had several pints too many he continued "Did you get married? Is she off working as a nanny somewhere again?"

"No, Fiona and I are not together any more" said Finn, in a flat voice.

"Ah!" said Jake, "I'm sorry to hear that, young man!"

"And the filum scripts? Not writing them now?" persisted Robin.

"No, you see" said Finn, remembering his briefing notes and forcibly making his vision of Fiona sink further down his mind, to stop it clouding his thoughts and tearing at his heart, as it always did when she was mentioned, "Fiona *went off with the Film Producer*! I got sacked and she got a new man! So I had to come home!"

'*If only*' Finn added to himself, 'but briefing notes do have their uses sometimes!'

---

[12] Little Wychwell 8 A cellist in the well

"Well, who'd have thought *that* might happen eh? Never know in life do you? Up one minute down the next! Still *it is what it is!*" said Jake.

"Yes" concurred Robin, nodding agreement "*It is what it is!* Never a wiser sentence spoken!"

"But I'm writing another book!" said Finn, continuing down his briefing notes on what to say if asked about his previous stay in Little Wychwell, "I'm expecting great success with this new one!"

'Did whoever wrote the briefing notes have to put *that* bit in?' Finn asked himself, 'And why did I say it myself? I hope I don't have to sit here pretending to type a book *again*! I had quite enough of that last time!'

Robin banged his empty glass down and looked at Finn hopefully, but Jake looked at the clock and shook his head at Robin.

"Robin, we had best get off home before Stinker discovers Finn has stayed open after hours. Don't want him to get told off or be thrown out of this job and board!" said Jake, "Will we be seeing you again tomorrow?"

"Could be!" said Finn.

"Looking forward to it!" said Jake, "You are a *true gentleman!*" he added, waving his hand vaguely towards the empty glasses.

Finn dashed round to the front of the bar to reunite them with their zimmer frame and stick and then Jake and Robin helped each other out of the Wyching Well and, very unsteadily, wove off homewards taking a line that wiggled from side to side of the road.

Upstairs Stinker, feeling peaceful and happy after playing his cello the entire evening, had tucked himself up in bed and fallen fast asleep.

Finn tiptoed upstairs and peeked in to see if Stinker needed sustenance but decided to leave him slumbering.

Finn could not be bothered to cook himself anything either although he was very hungry so instead he fortified himself with three bottles of a local craft brewery's milk stouts. Milk Stout sounded nourishing, Finn thought, and did not check the alcohol content. Finn finished washing the glasses, cleaned the bar, mopped the floor, unrolled his sleeping bag on one of the long oak benches and dropped into a milk stout induced deep sleep.

An hour later he was dreaming that Fiona had returned, let herself into the bar together with a blast of cold night air from the door, drifted quietly over to him and leaning down she had kissed him and then whispered softly in her beautiful honey heather voice, "Finn, it's me, wake up!"

The dream was so real that Finn jerked awake and sat bolt upright.

Fiona was not there but Flipper was and was choking himself to avoid laughing too loudly.

"Did you *pretend* to be *Fiona*?" Finn demanded crossly.

"I feel I have got her voice off pretty well now!" replied Flipper.

"Please tell me you didn't *kiss* me!" said Finn.

"Not at all!" replied Flipper, "You are not on my list of frogs whom I want to turn into princes""

"Good, that bit *was* just the dream!" said Finn.

"But I could have *killed* you!" said Flipper "What were you thinking of, *no alarms set up*?"

"Three craft brewery milk stouts and an evening working in the bar" said Finn, ruefully, "I have a terrible headache! I dread to think what they put in that stuff. How did you get in? I locked and barred the *front* door, I definitely remember doing that."

"I made a copy of the back door key last time I was in these parts" replied Flipper "Not just the alarms but you didn't remember to put the bolt on the back door! Should I recommend you for a refresher course in basic security and safety?"

"Only if you want me to retaliate by putting you on a course in not having affairs with agents from other countries!" retorted Finn.

"I can't have affairs!" said Flipper, "I'm dead![13]"

"Usual pathetic excuse from you!" said Finn, "Never known anyone milk the same excuse as much as you do! Just go behind the bar, put the kettle on and see if dead people can make me a black coffee if you are going to hang around any longer!"

"Just come to collect the photos off the camera!" said Flipper, "And I've already done that so I'll be off in a moment! Don't dream about *me* next! And bolt the back door behind me!"

With those words he was gone.

Finn was glad Flipper was back safe from wherever he had just been and was clearly his partner on this project even if he had been in an annoying mood. Finn reset the alarms from his sleeping bag but thought he would leave bolting the back door until he had just had a *little* bit more of a nap! It was quite safe in Little Wychwell, there was no need for Flipper to flap about like a landed fish! Flipper was right though, he had been culpably careless, but Flip wouldn't tell anyone else. He wondered if he should bolt the back door. But Finn's head was thumping, his mouth was dry, he could not be bothered attempting to stand up and move about. In only a few seconds he was fast asleep again.

At four thirty a.m. Finn's slumber was again rudely interrupted. A jolly tune played loudly in his ear. It was the movement alarm but would have sounded like a mobile phone to anyone else. Finn hastily sat upright, moving his hand to his gun, just in case.

"Oh good, you're awake!" said a strident high pitched female voice "How fortunate that your phone got a text just then! It would have been *so* tiresome to have to wake you up!"

Finn's eyes strained through the darkness of the bar and he made out the figure of a woman with very long dark hair and dark eyes who was less than five feet tall and insubstantially thin.

"Who are you?" Finn asked.

"Nimuë!" she replied, holding out her hand to shake his.

---

[13] All that Glisters is not Silver, Little Wychwell Three

"Finn!" said Finn, removing both his arms from his sleeping bag, wondering if he had forgotten who this woman was but being pretty convinced he had never seen her before.

"You must be the *barman*, I suppose!" said Nimuë, "It's very generous of Stinker to give you bed and board with the job, I gather accommodation is *very* expensive round here! I'm so glad he is doing well enough to have *staff* now!"

"Unusual name, Nimuë" said Finn, to avoid replying to her remarks.

"Yes, Arthurian legends are one of Poppa's academic specialities" said Nimuë.

"I presume this is a social call of some sort - it's rather early even for the most enthusiastic alcohol and bar products sales rep!" said Finn.

"Are you asking why am I *here*?" she responded, sounding as if she thought that was obvious, "You must know why I am here. Stinker must have told you! I'm *Stinker's girlfriend*!"

"You *are*?" asked Finn feeling that he could not have been more surprised if there had been a sudden earthquake in Little Wychwell. Stinker had never had a relationship that counted for more than a very brief flirtation with anyone as far as Finn knew.

"Oh yes! Defs! Although I haven't been his girlfriend *actively* for a while! I was Stinker's girlfriend when we were both at Coromandel!" replied Nimuë.

"You *were*?" said Finn, who was beginning to wonder if he might not still be asleep. At Coromandel College? That would have been years and years ago when they were all undergraduates!

"I read music like Stinker and played the cello too" she said.

"That seems a good basis for a compatible relationship" said Finn, thinking he was coping well with this very puzzling conversation. Stinker's girlfriends were usually very short lived. They soon became tired of trying to compete for attention with the music in his head. Another musician and cellist would seem more able to overcome that particular problem.

But even Finn could not believe that Stinker had been keeping this girl as a secret girlfriend ever since Oxford, although if she only ever appeared in his life at four thirty am in the morning Finn supposed this might have been possible.

"We only started going out together in the last three weeks of our final term of our final year and once we had finished taking Finals I went abroad on my gap experience because that was already arranged as a done thing before I went out with Stinker" she replied, "I have always meant to come back to him but I was having *such* a good time! I suppose we lost touch a teeny bit! But I was always, *always* his girlfriend!"

Hmmm, thought Finn, two out of touch with reality music students, the years rolling on and neither of them really noticing it, that was, he supposed, just about conceivable. But Stinker had had a few short lasting relationships since College and he found it impossible to believe that this girl had been alone all this time? Was she even who she *said* she was? Finn was beginning to wonder about this visitor and whether she was not A Person of Suspicion in the case which he was investigating.

"Out of interest, how did you get in?" he asked.

"Oh I've been here before, on the only other time I've been back to dear old England since Finals! I had almost forgotten about that visit myself! I popped back for two weeks and it happened to be *just* after Stinker bought this place. I saw he had bought it on social media and rushed round to see my dearest love! Of course he was aux anges to see me again, and I him, and he gave me a back door key, for the next time I called round and he wasn't there because I said I would be back the next day! But then I had this *perfectly marvellous opportunity* to go abroad again and I never came back here and I completely forgot I had his key! So I got back *again* yesterday and I just *happened* to find the key in one of my suitcases when I was unpacking my things at the Aging Parents House and I thought 'Why not pop round and see my loved one as soon as I finish unpacking?" she answered.

"You finished unpacking in the middle of the night and you thought you would just pop round and see Stinker *now*?" asked Finn.

"*Impulsive*! I've always been *impulsive*!" she replied, "Also a teeny bit confused about the time due to jet lag! I suddenly felt I *absolutely* had to see him. I wasn't expecting *you* to be here! Apologies for waking you instead of going straight upstairs to find him but I just need to sort something out before I meet up with Stinker again! I have a little errand for you! I want you to go and ask Stinker if he has admitted yet that I was right over a little bit of a dispute we had last time I was here."

"A little dispute last time you were here? Years ago? I can't see he will even remember *having* a dispute!" Finn replied.

"Oh he *will*" replied Nimuë, "We had a *mega* row about who was the best composer of all time. He would *not* give in. *Nor* would I. We were both *resolute*! I haven't communicated with him since then, not even by text."

Finn was still of the opinion that since Stinker was male he was most unlikely to even recall the event and also that Nimuë seemed to be making up stories as she went along.

"So you've been *working* abroad?" asked Finn.

"*Travelling*. I wander wherever the whim takes me. I like travelling. I have a huge allowance from the aging Ps so I can do whatever I like whenever I like wherever I like" she answered, "But after I found the key and I thought of Stinker...*guess what I thought next*?"

"*Hard to say*" replied Finn, who was feeling very glad that Nimuë was not *his* girlfriend although he could see that she and Stinker might be ideal for each other due to both being completely detached from real life.

"I decided, all in a millisecond, that it is *time for me to settle down*! I am going to *live here, marry Stinker and become a Pub Landlady*!" she said.

"Does Stinker know that?" asked Finn.

"No" Nimuë replied, giving Finn a smile so dazzling he blinked, "Don't tell him! I'll tell him myself! He will be *pleased*!"

Finn had not bothered to get undressed when he climbed into his sleeping bag. This meant he did not have to jump around the room wearing a sleeping bag so that he could go and get dressed in the gent's loos. He divested himself of the sleeping bag and pushed his hair back behind his ears.

"If you look behind the bar" Finn said, "you will find a kettle, coffee and at least two cups. Please put the kettle on and make me a cup of strong black coffee while I go and see if Stinker is awake."

"Over indulged on the alco? You *must* remember to tell him he *has* to agree that it's *Tallis* or else I will leave again, I will leave *immediately!*" said Nimuë looking surprisingly fierce. She stamped her foot hard on the floor.

Finn sincerely hoped that Stinker was not going to be difficult and insist the best composer ever was Vaughan Williams or Beethoven or anyone except Tallis as he did not think that Nimuë would take that news at all well and he, Finn, was not looking forward to being the person who delivered it to her.

"You know what" Finn said, suddenly inspired, "If you are going to marry him I think you had better be able to go and wake him and ask him about the composer yourself. Then I can make *myself* some coffee!"

Finn suddenly did not trust this girl, she had appeared here from 'abroad', just after Finn had arrived here himself. Was *anything* she said true? Finn kept everything he needed stowed in his rucksack and had it under his head when asleep so she could not have touched any of it. But he now wished he had bolted the back door.

"*Oh, oh, oh no*! I can't! *I just can't ask him myself*! What would I do if he disagreed. I would be desolate! *All my plans in ruins!*" she screamed at him, fell dramatically onto a chair and burst into loud tears.

They were saved from further debate about who would wake Stinker because the door to the stairs opened and Stinker himself appeared.

"Nimuë!" cried Stinker, "*Nimuë*! It is *you*! It's *really you*! I heard your voice from upstairs but I thought I was imagining it! I thought it was one of the dreams I have where you reappear! But you're *here*! You have come back! Nimuë, *it is Tallis*! You were right all along! I have thought about that so often, *all these years of regret on my part*, oh Nimuë, *please stop crying!*"

Nimuë sprang up off the chair with a huge smile. Her smile was triumphant thought Finn, not loving, he did not like this woman, although he admitted to himself that possibly that was because she had woken him up with such a start. At least some of what she had said to him was clearly perfectly true. Well, Finn could not stay here as a third person at a moving lover's reunion, there seemed little hope of getting breakfast *or* going back to sleep now.

Then Finn had an inspirational idea about where he could find coffee in Little Wychwell at that time of morning so he rolled up his sleeping bag, tucked it into the loops on his rucksack, shouldered the rucksack and said "Well, I'm off for a walk!"

Neither Stinker nor Nimuë noticed him leave. They were now holding hands and looking into each other's eyes. He had a feeling they might be about to burst into an operatic aria. Finn left hastily.

Finn knew where he would be welcome for breakfast and a chat! Elodea was always up at 5am and would have already brewed a big pot of coffee by the time he reached the Old Vicarage.

Chapter Three

About thirty minutes after Finn left the newly reunited lovers in the Wyching Well he was comfortably ensconced in the kitchen at the Old Vicarage with Elodea. Elodea was stylishly dressed in an extravagantly ornate black blouse embellished with sequins and a smart knee length bright red velvet skirt very suitable for any evening soiree. They were both eating bacon and fried bread sandwiches and oohing and aahing together over the exciting appearance of the previously unknown by them Nimuë. Elodea had been satisfactorily and properly impressed with the news and was not at all put out by Finn's appearance in her kitchen at that time of day.

Elodea also fully understood the need for coffee and bacon sandwiches after imbuing an excessive amount of milk stout on the previous evening.

"And you say that Nimuë looks rather like Stinker's description of Lady Therese?" Elodea was asking.

"Very small, thin, black hair, black eyes!" said Finn.

"Interesting *psychologically*! Perhaps he *was* asleep when he saw Lady Therese![14]" replied Elodea.

"Possible!" agreed Finn, "But either way, his real love and his phantom love appear to have strangely similar appearances!"

They both nodded wisely.

"It's funny that none of us have heard of her before!" said Elodea, "But maybe she was only here for a day or so when she came here the first time and collected that key. Maybe it wasn't two weeks, maybe not even a day? If Stinker was badly hurt when she disappeared again he would not have complained and moaned aloud, he would not have said anything at all, he would have just gone and played his cello sadly for hours."

"That is *also* true!" concurred Finn.

"And you say *she is going to marry him*?" asked Elodea.

---

[14] See Amare Valde, Little Wychwell 9

"So *she* says!" replied Finn.

They both chewed thoughtfully for a while, considering the implications of this new development while Grandson of Babe patted them alternately on the knee to get his share of their sandwiches.

"She seems to be from a quite well off family, she said she lived on an allowance from her parents, so she wouldn't be too much of an *expense* for him, she could support him financially perhaps?" said Finn.

"That might improve Stinker's life!" Elodea agreed, "Not that he appears to have any interest whatsoever in money provided he has enough to get by."

"Remind me" Finn said to Elodea, "Never *ever* to drink any local craft brewery milk stout *ever again*! I feel great now thanks to your bacon and coffee!"

"I don't suppose you will be wanting to continue sleeping on a bench in the Wyching Well if it's now turned into a Love Nest" said Elodea.

"Beggars can't be choosers" said Finn.

"But I've had a *wonderful* idea to solve that one!" said Elodea, "It just popped into my head! You know Clive Patterson, the Artist, only he calls himself something entirely different on his paintings? He lives in Wooky Place in Little Wychwell?"

"I can't say I do" said Finn, "But I have quite probably met him when I was in Little Wychwell before."

"Oh yes, I'm sure you have, he is often in the Wyching Well! A 'regular' as it were" said Elodea. "He paints abstracts, very, very good ones! He's quite noted in the Art World! I *love* his work myself!"

"Does he have a spare room he is trying to let?" asked Finn, hopefully.

"No, or at least he might do, I don't know. Just be quiet till I finish explaining my idea!" said Elodea holding a finger up to stop him speaking.

"So, a few years ago Clive accidentally burnt his studio down, he has a big studio in his garden you understand, it was something to do with oil paint and using a blowtorch to try to get it to dry faster. Now you would think he might have had more sense especially he must have been using oil paint for many years. However I know myself, from bitter experience with it, that oil paint can take *months* to dry, *literally* months in the old fashioned meaning of literal, I do not *exaggerate*. So perhaps the disaster was not just due to being so artistic he floats around in another world a lot of the time! He may have had a commission to deliver that was simply not going to dry in time?" continued Elodea.

"Man with a tweed jacket and a shirt with spots of multicoloured paint on it in places? I'm *right*, aren't I?" asked Finn, with a note of triumph in his voice. Finn had been reviewing possible Clives from the collection of villagers in the Wyching Well on the previous evening and had not listened to anything Elodea said after the words 'burnt his studio down'.

"Yes, yes, that's *him*! But *shush* till I have *finished*!" said Elodea, "*Pay attention*!"

Elodea continued, "To resume! When Clive's studio was destroyed in the fire he lost a lot of his work of course and some of it was commissions with deadlines so he couldn't wait to repaint them until after the studio was rebuilt So, I and John, well *me*, but John *agreed*, said he could use one of our outhouses for a bit, even if it wasn't ideal. He had a look and said it 'would do' which seemed a bit ungrateful at the time given that we were letting him have it for free. But naturally artists are fussy about where they work, they need the right conditions. However he turned out to be a *very* good rent free tenant and we were sorry we had thought he was ungrateful. You see he paid to have our outhouse redecorated and refurbished and even put a loo and a huge sink in for washing his brushes and he rewired all the electricity and put lots of power points in and even an electric storage heater. So that when he moved out again we got all those improvements for free for our own use! So instead of being an old decaying outhouse it's a perfectly habitable little studio now!"

Finn said, finally seeing the point, "So, it's the sort of place someone could use to sleep in?"

"Yes, and *even better*, it has its own door out on to the road, so you don't need to go in and out through the garden or come anywhere near this house!" Elodea finished.

"Yes, this could certainly solve the problem!" said Finn "I can still go and help Stinker out by doing the bar at the Wyching Well in the evenings and he and Nimuë can have some time together alone while she is here. But...you *have* to ask John first!"

Elodea pouted, "But you will not be *in* this house, John only said you were not allowed *in this house*!"

"And naturally I *never* enter the house *ever* now!" said Finn.

They both laughed.

"But you *must* ask him!" Finn persisted.

"I *suppose*!" said Elodea, a little grumpily, "Do you want to see the Studio first?"

They trotted out together across the lawn.

It was a not very big but adequate although it still had some easels and part finished paintings in it.

"Not bad!" said Finn, looking at one of the half-finished paintings and wondering if perhaps the word Abstract meant something else in the Art World now.

"These paintings are not *Clive's* obviously!" said Elodea, "I'm afraid that is just me making rather a mess and wasting paint!"

"They are not at all bad!" said Finn, politely, "That one of Barnabus and Angel and the children is really good!"

"I just do a bit of dabbling to make presents for people" said Elodea, "I expect they probably put them in the bin or the attic or the downstairs loo or something but it amuses me and if I do them for presents I feel like I am not just wasting money on the materials or wasting time by amusing myself in a selfish way! There is nothing important here, you can just put the easels on one side while you are here!"

There was, as Elodea had said, a door out to the road on the other side of the Studio with a huge Victorian key hung on a peg beside it.

"Is there a key to the door into the door we just entered by as well?" asked Finn.

"There must be one somewhere but once you are in here you can bolt it on the inside, it's also a very old door and has massive bolts" said Elodea, "Besides no one is likely to come in that way from the garden!"

Finn thought that he *trusted* not but after looking at the bolts he had to agree that they were very sturdy and probably more protection from unwanted intruders than most door keys offered.

"*Pretty much perfect*! Thank you so much! I am truly grateful for your offer!" he said, "But *only* if John says it's OK with him!"

"I'll ask! I *promise*!" said Elodea.

"I'd best be off before John gets down, I don't want to upset him before you even ask him! I think I might go and sit up a tree for a while. I like sitting up trees. It's *peaceful*! No cellists up trees!" said Finn.

Finn faded out of the room in the unexpected way he always did. Elodea looked round towards where he had been standing and he had simply gone.

Elodea smiled. She had enjoyed this chat with Finn, she thought of him and Flipper as extra children of her own when they were about. If Finn moved into the studio he could pop in for a chat regularly and update her on how the Nimuë situation was playing out in the Wyching Well and hear all the village gossip he picked up from behind the bar too! She wondered for a moment why Finn was here and then dismissed it from her mind. She always felt a sadness about both Finn and Flipper, they always had a sort of barrier of loneliness around them, they were unable to take part in normal life due to their work. They were always forced to view the worst of human nature, always trying to keep others safe before themselves and yet even having to kill sometimes to save others.

Finn wandered back to the Big Oak. He sat up there for an hour or two in insect ridden peace for Cyril was out raiding all the bird tables in the village. Nothing happened at all around the White House. Finn felt it was deserted and yet it gave a realistic impression of not being deserted. It was quite true that lights went on and off and sounds were heard from outside as if people were moving around inside and yet Finn felt in his soul that the house was empty of life. Automatic system, he said to himself, but a very clever one.

Finn was very comfortable and very full of bacon and coffee, the birds had got over being momentarily startled at his appearance and were singing beautifully, a light breeze ruffled the leaves, he was content.

'I wonder why humans ever came down from living in trees?" he mused to himself, "It's perfect up here!"

Just at that moment of bliss he spied a large grey furry shape running along the telegraph wires further along the road, Cyril was heading back home.

"Ah, time to leave!" Finn told himself and hastily shinned down the trunk, "I'll go and see if Stinker needs help opening up!"

When he reached the Wyching Well there was a powerful smell of skunk drifting out of the upstairs window. When he got into the bar the smell drifting down the stairs and through the open door into the bar was even worse.

Stinker was in the bar, lethargically polishing the beer taps.

"Stinker!" said Finn "Is Nimuë smoking something she shouldn't?"

"It's only herbal cigarettes!" said Finn, "She's trying to give up smoking tobacco!"

"Herbal! *Illegally herbal*! You must know perfectly well what it is! Has she bewitched you or something? You can smell it in the street. The whole of Little Wychwell will be talking about it by now! Do you want the local Police round here?" said Finn.

"Do you think they worry about it these days?" asked Stinker.

"Given all the things you worry about being shut down for I am surprised you even ask!" said Finn, "Tell her to only *swallow* illegal things in future if she must take them! I hope she didn't give you a puff?"

"It would be my own business if she had!" said Stinker grumpily, then he relented, smiled at Finn and said, "You know I don't do illegal drugs! Once a top rower always a top rower!"

"Not sure anyone told our *Second* Eight that one!" said Finn.

"Which is why they were not the *First* Eight!" said Stinker, "Same at Coromandel!"

They gave each other a high five and were friends again.

"Well, if you are that worried about her smoking in here, I'll go and tell her. But I warn you, she won't like it!" said Stinker.

"And you won't like being closed down either!" said Finn, determined to win this one.

Stinker trotted upstairs, there were a few loud screeches from above and then he came back down.

"OK I told her! I had to say it was OK if she ate cannabis in food instead though" he said, "She says she *needs* to take it for medicinal reasons."

"It doesn't *do* anything medically, that's only a *myth!*" said Finn.

"*Whatever!* Lots of people think it has good properties even if it's a placebo effect and even some medics think it does. I didn't realise how far gone Nimuë is on sampling drugs though. She never used to be *quite* this bad at Oxford. She has been telling me that she has tried things like Mescalin and every other local drug she ever met on her travels. She says it helps her to a higher plane for her music and that is most important, achieving a spiritual connection to the music, *being* the music! I can wander off into *being* the music without any external help but not everyone can. Nimuë takes the drugs to achieve that state. No wonder she never remembered to get in touch with me though with all the things she has been swallowing and smoking! I expect she did not notice the time was passing! Even though it has been so many years!" said Stinker,

"But, don't worry, now she is back here with me I am going to wean her off them and save her!"

Finn wished him good luck with that hopeless task, but he did not say it aloud.

Stinker stopped talking and sniffed. He looked around vaguely and considered the smell of the air in the bar, then he snapped to attention, "Finn! *The air*! You are right! Shut the door to the stairs and help me get all the other windows and doors open! I hadn't realised what a fug there is down here because it's so much worse upstairs it seemed clear down here! Can we get rid of it by opening time do you think?"

"If we open the back and front doors and hope there is a through breeze" said Finn, "We could try blaming it on the next-door neighbours?"

"Not at their age surely? They are well past retirement! We could suggest they are taking it for medicinal reasons? Or that they were hippies when they were younger? I *know*, we'll say we *hadn't noticed it at all* if anyone should ask" said Stinker, "Then everyone else can just *imagine* it's coming *in* from next door and not *out* from here!"

"That's a hopeful idea on your part!" said Finn, "But it seems the best strategy under the circumstances!"

They opened all the doors and the windows that had not been jammed shut for decades and Stinker tore a large piece of cardboard from the side of a wine delivery box and began to rather ineffectually flap it around to try to move the air faster.

With the air clearing Finn felt he could tackle the next subject, *"Living arrangements!"* announced Finn, "Now that Nimuë is here I feel rather like a gooseberry so I'm going to move in to the Studio in Elodea's garden, provided John agrees and Elodea is so forceful I can't see *that* being a problem. I'll be back here every evening for the next few weeks though so you can have your evenings free with Nimuë while you both get to know each other again!"

"Oh Finn, you're a *rock*!" said Stinker, "I don't know that I've ever had a *bro*' to look out for me before, no one has ever had my back like you do!"

Stinker had tears of emotion in his eyes. Finn thought that with a speech like that either Nimuë must have given Stinker a few puffs or else Stinker had inhaled too much sidestream smoke.

Finn was feeling annoyed about Nimuë's smoking habits himself. It was *essential* not to have the Police hanging around and popping in to check up on the Wyching Well as that would make the sort of people who might have helpful information for him run a mile. What a *nuisance* the girl was! Why had she turned up *now*? Was she one of the people whom he sought? He couldn't *quite* see an artistic drug addicted upper class sibarite like Nimuë as a master criminal but then if master criminals were that easy to spot Finn wouldn't have a job.

"You know I am *so happy*, so happy *she is back*, but, Finn, I'd forgotten, she *scares* me a bit too! She always has! She is quite, erm, quite difficult to *oppose*. Do you think, do you think we have a *future together*?" asked Stinker.

"Of course you do! Get on with you! You are just scared of *commitment*!" soothed Finn, who had not foreseen that Stinker might not be completely enthusiastic about Nimuë returning and having just relabelled her as a possible suspect Finn now wanted to keep her where he could see her.

"Nimuë" said Finn, "Unusual name!"

"Her father is an Arthurian scholar" said Stinker.

"Ah yes, so she said" replied Finn, "What was it Nimuë was in the legends exactly?"

"The Arthurian legends vary because they *are* legends I suppose" replied Stinker, "Nimuë may be The Lady of the Lake who produced the Sword, she was both Arthur's helper and also, in a way, his doom. But probably more likely to be another name for Viviane, the nymph who entranced and captured Merlin, entombed him in rock, stole his magical knowledge and weakened him to death. I know because I have always planned to compose a piece based on the legends but I never quite get round to it."

"I suppose" Finn said to Stinker, "that you don't have Arthur or Lancelot or anything like that as any of your names?"

"No!" said Stinker, "But just a minute! I'll check! Just in case I have forgotten one of them! I'm so confused with Nimuë returning, delirium of happiness and all that stuff and also I hardly ever use them all or hear anyone else say them. Here we go!"

Stinker stood very formally as if he was giving a speech and recited out loud, "My name is Anthony St Crispin Alexander Clement Stinkwater Fitzdemetre, no, nothing Arthurian in there!"

"Good!" said Finn, thinking any delirium was not due to happiness but more the delirium of illegal side stream smoking.

"Do you have any Arthurian names?" asked Stinker.

"No" said Finn, "But I'm not going out with an Arthurian enchantress so it wouldn't matter if I did!"

"But if the name is another name for Viviane it was *Merlin* who Nimuë enchanted and trapped not Lancelot or Arthur" said Stinker.

"Yes, I stand corrected, you are right! You aren't called *Merlin* either?" replied Finn.

"Ah! But that one was a very call, my Mother was *very* keen on calling me Merlin but my Father stopped her! You don't think that *counts* do you, *nearly* being called Merlin?" asked Stinker, nervously.

"I trust not!" replied Finn.

To distract Stinker from Arthurian connections, as he seemed to be taking these ideas far too seriously, Finn continued "There's something I just *have* to ask though, I couldn't help noticing the resemblance between Nimuë and your description of Lady Therese in your requiem mass. *Does* Nimuë look like Lady Therese?"

"*Does Nimuë look like Lady Therese*?" asked Stinker, sounding most surprised. He stopped to consider.

Then Stinker said, "No! *Not at all*. Similar colouring, OK *very* similar colouring, and long hair too and the same sort of *size* I suppose but...no! Entirely different faces! Different characters. Different ages too but ....*no, definitely not*! They are entirely *different tunes*."

"They are different *tunes*?" asked Finn.

"Yes, everyone has their own tune, I always hear them when I meet a person, it's quite easy to hear them if you are quiet yourself and listen!" replied Stinker.

"I see!" said Finn, thinking he must remember to tell Elodea that their theory about Lady Therese being Nimuë was completely blown when he saw her. Also that Stinker classified people by their personal tunes which he thought everyone else could hear too if they only listened. Elodea would be *delighted* with that idea, she could ask Stinker what her own tune was the next time she met him. Finn thought he had better not ask what *his* own tune might be in case it was too disappointing.

But it was too late, Stinker was already explaining Finn's own tune, "This is *your* tune Finn, *listen*! It encompasses so many things "the rhythm of the oars, the river lapping the shore, hard work, order, duty, the world of fresh air and nature, the rhythm of life, the rhythm of the Planet itself!"

Stinker hummed a rather erratic sequence of just ten notes. When he finished Finn looked at him rather blankly, having already forgotten what the notes had been.

"Listen *again*! Listen *much harder*, close your eyes!" said Stinker and hummed the same notes several times.

Finn closed his eyes and listened more carefully. He saw the river, he felt the oars in his hands, he felt the regularity, the rhythm, the bow waves splashing the banks, the smell of the water, the feeling of eight people working as one together. He felt himself rising in the air, high above the river, up through the clouds, out into space from where he could see the whole of Planet Earth working as a regular and organized whole. He kicked himself mentally, "Get a grip, this is just *autosuggestion*!" he told himself, "those ten notes do not say *any* of that! Stinker said all of that, not the notes!" But he thought he had better humour Stinker.

"Ah!" said Finn, "Yes, definitely, entirely me! *Totally me!*"

"Absolutely *it is you*!" said Stinker.

"Oh yes, *completely me*! Well, that's *amazing*! Right, I'll be back to take over the bar at 7 o'clock. Just got to go and settle in at Elodea's!" said Finn.

Finn dashed out of the door before Stinker hummed anyone else's tune for him, he feared that Stinker's *own* tune might be an entire symphony and that he would have to listen to *all* of it.

Finn trotted along the road hoping that John had agreed about the Studio and that Stinker's head had fully cleared from its sidestream smoking session by the time he returned. The afternoon customers would not notice any oddities in Stinker's conversation as they all thought Stinker was eccentric to the point of insanity anyway.

Outside Robin and Jake were slowly progressing down the street in front of him, heading for the shop before coming back to the Wyching Well for their pints later.

"Cor, dear, what a whiff! Has our ol' Stinker taken up with drugs now?" said Robin as they passed the Wyching Well.

"No, he'd *never* do that! Used to be in the First Eight, see! At least so he always says! But I gather that's Stinker's long-lost girlfriend has reappeared. From what I recall of her I expect she is smoking a quick spliff!" said Jake.

"Long lost *girlfriend*?" asked Robin.

"Don't you remember? One appeared soon after Stinker first arrived and then vanished. I seem to recall he said they had some kind of a musical row." said Jake.

"A *musical row*?" asked Robin, laughing, "What's a *musical* row? He blew a trumpet at her and she blew a tuba back at him?"

"No idea! But I suppose music is safer than most martial arts!" said Jake, "Anyway, *she's back*!"

"*Back*?" asked Robin, "What? Just reappeared *after all these years*?"

"Yes, she come back *in the night*. Young Roland was just passing here, having been out" Jake stopped and gave a meaningful cough, then he lowered his voice "He was night shooting *rabbits*!"

"Ah" said Robin, "Big rabbits that look a bit like deer? Has he got a bit of venison spare for me?"

"He will have, he will have!" said Jake, "Anyway this car comes up behind him right here, going far too fast, so, thinking it might be the cops, he fades into the hedge with his *rabbits*" and here Jake coughed again "so the car and the driver don't see him!"

"And?" said Robin.

"Well, to his surprise the car screeches to a halt outside the Wyching Well. So he's stuck there, in the hedge because if he moves they will see him. There the car is now! Some car eh?" said Jake.

"*Very* tasty car!" said Robin.

"And out this woman gets and looks in her bag like she's lost something" said Robin, "Then she says 'Oh here it is!', waves a big key around and bounces off round the back of the Wyching Well. Our Roland got himself out of the hedge and off down the road before she came back out again and saw him."

"How did he know it was the same girl as went out with Stinker before?" asked Robin.

"Once seen never forgotten!" said Jake, "*You'll* remember her when you *see* her! She's a bit of a looker! Called Nina or something! Posh chick!"

"I'll look forward to seeing her in that case!" said Robin.

***

"Did you ask John yet?" Finn texted to Elodea as he headed back to the Old Vicarage.

"Yes, of course!" she texted back.

"And what did he say?" asked Finn.

"He said *fine*" replied Elodea.

"Are you sure he was listening when you asked?" texted Finn.

"Well really!" texted Elodea "As if I would take advantage of the fact he was working and ask him when he wasn't listening!"

She added an angry emoji to the end of her text.

"Sorry! Much apologies!" replied Finn, while thinking that was just what Elodea *would* do.

"I assure you that John was listening and he was *not at all pleased*. But he said he supposed if we got blown up it would save him having to continue to try to organise collaborative projects with the Chemistry Department and that had about the same risk of being blown up as you being around does so he might as well agree. But you are *not allowed in the house*!" Elodea replied.

"Thank you!" texted Finn, thinking that Elodea not only talked without stopping for breath but also texted without stopping for breath "On my way to the Studio now!"

"I'll bring a tin of cake over!" Elodea replied, "And coffee and cups! Oh, look at the time! I'll bring sandwiches too!"

Finn feared he might lose his figure if he stayed in the Studio for too long, he had better get Flipper to deliver some weights next time he called in.

Chapter Four

Finn was pleased with his new sanctuary at the Old Vicarage. He was used to surviving without comforts and this new pad had a leakless roof, a kettle, a sink and toilet and even heating!

He went back to the Wyching Well at six thirty pm feeling that his accommodation problem was now well and truly fixed.

But when he got to the Wyching Well there was no Stinker behind the bar, just a set of rather discontented customers on the other side.

"Hooray! Here comes the calvary!" said Alf Bartlett.

"What?" said Finn, "Where's Stinker?"

"Pops down every now and then and throws some drinks at us and off he goes upstairs again" said Alf, "We don't like to imagine what he is a doing off upstairs! Seems to involve a great deal of, er, noise, that's all I can say."

There was loud laughter from all.

"Well" said Finn, "*I'm* here now! Any Orders please?"

But no one seemed to be needing a drink just then and since most of the glasses were full it was clear that the customers had been helping themselves for free in Stinker's absence. Although generally a very honest village it has to be admitted that the local Little Wychwell moral rule book included the concept that a deliberately unattended bar meant that any drinks to which you helped yourself were free of charge. Stinker knew that fact himself too for he had warned Finn about this habit and told him not to leave the room except for the briefest possible time.

Finn put the TV on and got the customers focussed on shouting out the answers to an early evening quiz program. This gave Finn an opportunity to start to process the huge pile of unwashed glasses through the glass cleaning machine.

"Stinker doesn't have the sense he was born with" Finn grumbled to himself, "Whatever attractions Nimuë has to offer he cannot afford to lose so much money!"

But now that the customers were quieter Finn realised that the sound floating down from upstairs was not lovemaking but singing, wordless singing, , a beautiful sound, bewitching, enchanting, the song of the sirens. He felt it filling his mind and taking it over. He felt drawn towards it.

"What a fabulous voice Nimuë has!" Finn said aloud, without even intending to do so.

He got a grip on himself, "Wake up!" he said sternly to himself "Singing is only wailing by another name!"

There was a pause in the singing.

Then Stinker's cello repeated the same wonderful wordless song.

Then there was another pause.

Then the singing and the cello repeated the same sounds as a duet.

'I suppose neither of them need feeding?' Finn asked himself 'I don't think I need to cook for them. I've put plenty of food in the fridge and she could always take her car and go and get a pizza or something if she doesn't like any of it! She has enough money! I was going to do something quick for Stinker and myself before I started work but that's out now.'

Finn found and stuffed in a bag of his favourite crisps and then the drinks orders began to roll in.

But although Stinker must have been able to hear how busy it was downstairs Stinker never appeared in the bar for the rest of the evening. Nimuë crooning followed by the cello crooning, followed by combined crooning, went on and on and on. Finn no longer found this entrancing but torturous. 'It seemed beautiful when I *first* heard it' Finn said to himself, 'but I bet the sailors got jolly tired of the mermaids singing at them very soon after they jumped off their boats and on to those rocks, the mermaids probably didn't drown them, they probably drowned themselves to escape from the noise!"

The evening wore on. Nothing of interest seemed to be being discussed by the locals other than the recent football matches. Finn decided to just observe the social relationships between the customers before attempting to instigate active investigative discussions. He leant against the back of the bar and ate another bag of crisps.

This time Finn removed everyone forcibly and promptly at closing time so that the bar was clear just after midnight. Once Finn had thrown the last customers out he decided that Stinker could put the rest of the pile of dirty glasses through the glasses cleaner and do the floor himself. Finn was now grumpy. He had spent a whole evening running the bar without finding out any interesting facts while suffering a noise attack from above. The customers did not seem to mind the upstairs sounds much, although one of them did remark that it sounded like a cow calving and another said, no, he felt it was rather more like the noises made by a panicking flock of sheep if foxes got into the flock in the lambing season.

Once he had plodded wearily back to the Old Vicarage Finn was delighted to discover on his return to the Studio that Elodea and John had carried a bed from the house down to the Studio during his absence and left it made up with a full set of bed linen and a 'Good Night' tray of coffee and biscuits and fruit with cereal and milk for the morning too. Finn's good temper returned, how fortunate he was to have such kind hosts!

Finn had a restful night's sleep with no unexpected visitors. After considering the matter Finn decided he had better pop into the Wyching Well at ten a.m. to see if Stinker was up and about yet. Then he could tidy up from the night before if Stinker had *not* reappeared. He had now forgiven Stinker for his preoccupation, after all Finn had been in love himself and knew how distracting it could be and FInn could imagine a girl like Nimuë was *very* exacting in her demands on Stinker's time.

Finn expected to find the bar completely silent and peaceful as the lovers would be sleeping off their passion, or composing, or however you liked to label it. He was looking forward to peace and tranquility while he cleaned the place up. But he was sadly disappointed to find that the wailing, and then the wailing cello, and then the duet of wailing voice and cello were still continuing.

Finn found a pair of earplugs in his rucksack and inserted them. Wearing earplugs was absolutely not allowed when on active duty in an insecure place but there were limits to Finn's tolerance and madness seemed worse than a minor rule infringement.

At noon Stinker staggered down the stairs. His face was ashen and he looked utterly exhausted.

"Oh!" Stinker said, "You're *here*! Good!"

"Yes" said Finn, hastily removing his earplugs when he saw Stinker, "Just as well! We open in half an hour!"

Finn was surprised by his own use of the word "We" and realised, to his horror, that, after just two days on the bar, he was beginning to feel parochially attached to both the Wyching Well and its customers. "I must remember it's *not* mine, I *don't* work here and I *don't* live in this confounded village" he told himself severely.

"Sorry I'm so late! I've been *busy*!" said Stinker, "I'm, I'm *thirsty*! I think I am anyway!"

Stinker grabbed a half litre bottle of lemonade and drank it in one draft.

"Are you *OK*?" asked Finn.

"Finn, I *love* music, you *know* I love music, but Nimuë has forgotten how to compose to manuscript and I so I am having to help her to re-learn this skill. So she sings something, I write it down, then I play it on the cello to make sure it is exactly as she wants, then we sing and play it again together! She is composing a *huge* work of her own, I am not composing, only helping! I had forgotten how *entrancing* her voice is, so *very* beautiful. We have been working on her masterpiece since mid afternoon yesterday! But I *cannot* take a break in case she loses focus and I am *so* tired now!" said Stinker.

'Mid afternoon!' thought Finn to himself, 'No wonder the customers were *happy* when I arrived and didn't mind the 'noises off', three or four hours of free drinks!'

"So could you, could you possibly manage the bar this afternoon as well as this evening!" Stinker continued, "I *must* go back, *I must not stifle her genius*!"

"But Stinker" said Finn, "She must have done composition at Oxford, she took the same degree course that you did! *And* she can play the cello herself too!"

"I *suppose*!" said Stinker "But that's a long time ago and she says she has *forgotten*. Swallowing too many illegal things maybe? But she has not forgotten how to compose if she sings the music! When she sings it is like an enrapturing spell, so wonderful, even if she could transcribe the notes to paper format she could hardly write it all down at the same time as singing it could she?"

"Hmmm!" said Finn, "Don't you think if you can remember it to write it down then she can remember it?"

"I suppose, I don't know, perhaps not when she is in flow, she is composing, I am listening you see! I know that I *must* help her! This music *must not be lost to the World*!" replied Stinker.

Finn thought, after having heard it for a few hours himself, that the World might be better without it but he decided not to argue.

Finn looked at his friend. In just one day Stinker had changed from a reasonably happy, slightly plump, contented person to a grey faced, barely functional person whose fingers and arms were shaking.

"And what is Nimuë doing now?" asked Finn.

"Oh Nimuë is *asleep* now, she fell asleep suddenly, just after I had said I thought I heard you here running the glasses cleaner. But I *cannot* rest myself, I have to go back up and rewrite all my scraps of manuscript and notes of her composition into one *glorious coherent manuscript*!" said Stinker.

"You are going to do nothing of the sort!" said Finn, "You are going to sit right there at that table and I will go and get you some breakfast and you will *eat* it! What is she trying to do to you? Kill you?"

"*Do to me*? Nothing harmful, she loves me! It does not matter if I am worn away, I realise now that I could never compose at all, I just *thought* I could, I must diminish and she must increase! Oh I forgot to tell you some really wonderful news, we are getting married next month!" said Stinker, "Wish me happiness!"

"Wonderful!" said Finn, in whose mind the words 'Nimuë refused to give Merlin her love until he had taught her all his secrets' had just popped up. Finn told himself that he was being completely ridiculous and continued, very firmly, "Now sit down right there and I will get you some breakfast cooked before we have to open!"

Finn had just had a terrible vision of Stinker dying from exhaustion on him before Finn had solved the case. More words floated across his mind 'after Nimuë stole Merlin's secrets she entombed him, sealed away for ever'. 'Total tripe!' Finn told himself severely, 'This is nothing to do with the Arthurian legends, it's just that awful caterwauling affecting my brain! Or perhaps I am hungry too! Food, that's the solution to so many problems in this life!'

Finn sat Stinker firmly down on a chair and went and made both of them fried egg sandwiches and coffee in the tiny kitchen.

When he returned with the food Stinker was fast asleep sitting on the chair with his head leaning on his arms on the table. He did not stir at all even though Finn waved the sandwich and coffee right under his nose.

"Oh well!" said Finn, "Waste not want not!". He ate Stinker's sandwiches and coffee as well as his own.

He was just about to unlock the Wyching Well door to let the customers in when a fury descended the stairs and shook Stinker hard.

"What are you doing *asleep*?" Nimuë demanded and added "I have *felt more inspiration*, I must *continue*!"

Stinker blearily opened his eyes.

Nimuë hoicked Stinker out of the chair and dragged him by force back up the stairs.

"Coming!" Stinker said, weakly, as his feet banged on each step while she heaved him upwards lying prone on his back.

Finn noted that Nimuë might be very small but she clearly had muscles like iron. Stinker was not a small person to drag up those stairs. Then Finn wondered for how long you could survive on a half litre of lemonade, even if it was full sugar. What a shame Flipper was not there too, Flipper would have found the sight of Stinker being heaved around by Nimuë so very funny!

Finn unlocked the main door and let Alf and Robin and Jake in and then realised Flipper had *also* materialised in the garden and was waving through the back window pane out of view of the customers.

Finn gathered up a bag of rubbish. He gave his three customers a very strong lecture on what would happen if he found any drinks had disappeared in his absence because Stinker was not made of money and they did not want the Wyching Well to close. Then Finn popped out to the back pretending to go to the bin.

"Got your new pad's key?" Flipper hissed, "I need to make an impression of it so I can make a copy!"

"Is that *all* you are here for? You have *abandoned* me here to live in a huge crowd of lunatics instead of witnesses[15] and you have just popped in for a few seconds to get an impression of my new key?" hissed Finn back.

"Yep!" said Flipper, heartlessly, pressed the both sides of the key into some wax and vanished again over the back fence.

Finn sighed. He wished Flipper would have stayed for longer, he would have liked the company. Finn had been on trying missions before and thought this one was going to be a doddle but it was getting worse by the day what with gigantic squirrels, trilling women, insane composers, customers!

Finn remembered to put the rubbish bag into the bin and returned to the bar. Alf and Robin and Jake were sitting there looking very innocent with their glasses at the same level that Finn thought had been in them when he left. Finn decided they could not have filched more than one pint each

---

[15] Hebrews 12 v 1

in that time. Finn put a twenty pound note into the till himself just in case they had.

An hour or two later a very tall and very glamorous lady tottered in on excessively high heels, wearing very elaborate and ruffled occasion-wear.

"Maybe Elodea is not the only one who is wearing her old stock of clothes out!" Finn thought.

The new customer leant on the bar and said "Hello *Handsome!*" to Finn in a surprisingly deep voice.

Finn realised who it was and glared at her.

"Morgan le Fake" purred the customer, "I'm a *foreigner* to this area. I've travelled to your cute little village all the way from *Oxford!*"

The customer made Oxford sound as if it was thousands of miles away.

Finn felt despair clutching at his soul. For the new customer was *definitely* Flipper in the guise of a drag queen.

What was Flipper up to now? Could things get much worse? Finn had Stinker playing the fool upstairs and Flipper playing the fool downstairs. What next?

Finn served 'Morgan' the gin and slim line tonic with plenty of ice and slices of lemon and a straw that Morgan had ordered, all beautifully presented in a big balloon glass. Finn was *really* looking forward to seeing Flipper try to drink *that* with a straight face.

"Don't monopolise the *lady!*" said Alf, "Come on me dear, come and sit along of us!"

"*Told him* to get his eyes tested!" said Jake.

"What?" said Alf, who was not just short sighted these days but also rather deaf.

"*Coming* over!" simpered Morgan le Fake and minced over to their table.

Soon the four of them were having a raucous time together.

"I say" called Alf to Finn, "Morgan's going to be a new customer for you! She's hoping to move into Little Wychwell!"

"Super!" said Finn, not sounding at all enthusiastic. Finn felt he had enough customers without having to serve Flipper in the guise of a fake drag queen. Although, thought Finn, if he got to keep watching Flipper having to drink gin and tonics with a straw it would *almost* be worth it.

But truthfully Finn felt glad that Flipper was there. But why did Flipper choose *that* particular drag name? Finn didn't like to start sounding superstitious but he already had 'Stinker almost called Merlin' and Nimuë who bore a striking resemblance to the Arthurian one to deal with without Flipper deciding to take on the role of Morgan le Fay. Any moment now, he thought, *any* moment now, either Arthur or Lancelot will walk in.

But it wasn't either Arthur or Lancelot who came in next but Barnabus who had been allowed out for an hour by Angel. He smiled at Finn, ordered a pint of coca cola and leant comfortably against the bar. A few moments later he looked less happy.

"*What*" he murmured to Finn, "Is that ghastly noise from upstairs? Has Stinker got himself some strange form of pet bird? A macaw or something?"

"It's a bird but of the human variety" whispered Finn, "Noise? Hardly notice it myself already. It's like living near a railway line, you blot it out from your ears after a while."

Barnabus gave him a quizzical look, "Come on! Explain!" he said.

"Well, if you *must* know, it's Nimuë composing Music with Stinker's help, she can't manage to compose without. She is Stinker's old flame from Oxford and they are going to get married shortly" Finn replied.

"Yes, so Mama said" replied Barnabus, sotto voce,"I thought Mama might have lost it. Or that maybe you were telling her big fibs for some reason best known to yourself! Mama is terribly taken with the Romance of it All". Then Barnabus added, after a very piercing high note hit his eardrum, "Does this noise ever stop?"

"Hard to say. The mind clouds over after being exposed to it for long" replied Finn, "It's been like this for days and days I think! Maybe even months! Or is it just since yesterday? What can I get you to drink?"

Barnabus turned to find a place to sit and his eyebrows shot up at the sight of Morgan le Fake with Jake, Robin and Alf, "Who is *that*?" he hissed at Finn, "Are we in an alternative universe suddenly?".

Then Morgan looked directly at him and smiled and Barnabus recognised Flipper.

"*What is he playing at*?" Barnabus whispered to Finn.

"Don't ask me!" Finn answered, "I'm ignoring him!"

"Oh well, might as well go and sit with him I suppose! Maybe I'll find out why he's playing the fool like that!" whispered Barnabus.

Barnabus collected a chair from beside the bar and went and joined Morgan and Jake and Robin and Alf at their table, the others introduced him to Morgan le Fake.

"Interesting name" said Barnabus to Morgan, having heard all about Nimuë from Elodea, "I assume it's after Morgan le Fay of Arthurian legend? But did you know Little Wychwell has a *connection* to King Arthur?"

"No!" simpered Morgan, "How *wonderful*! I absolutely *must* move into the place *a s a p*! *How* is it connected?"

"There is an old legend in the village that the well right here, *at the Wyching Well*, is where Merlin was imprisoned by the Enchantress Nimuë and driven mad till he died" said Barnabus, "I remember hearing about it after" he lowered his voice, "...after a certain previous landlord...ahem...*fell* into it and sadly drowned![16] We never let Stinker, who is the Landlord here now, know about that little incident in case it upsets him!"

Robin and Jake and Alf nodded solemnly.

---

[16] Cellist in the Well, Little Wychwell 8

"Stinker must never be told about that!" said Jake, "Ever! We all agreed as we would not tell him because he might be spooked and then we might not have a pub! You know, these artistic types. Easily shaken!"

Finn, listening to their chatter from behind the bar, suddenly shivered for no reason. This mission was getting too spookily muddled up with Arthurian legend, even for a hardened sceptic like him. He hoped no-one had told Stinker *that* particular local myth about the Wyching Well being the place where Nimue had imprisoned Merlin.

"Oooh!" breathed Morgan le Fake seductively, "Hearing about that makes me go *all quivery*! You think Merlin might actually be *here*? Right here! Still sealed in? Underneath the floor?"

She gave a very suggestive gasp.

"More underneath the garden I would think. It is a wonderfully attractive idea, isn't it?" said Barnabus, "But sadly there seems to be no factual basis for it, although the Well here may have really been a holy shrine in Roman Britain, maybe pagan, maybe Christian, maybe pagan converted to Christian, so I suppose it's possible that Arthur or Merlin might have made a pilgrimage here to visit the well and drink the Holy Waters."

"Oooh!" breathed Morgan le Fake again, "I do *hope* so! I hope they both came here, even if not still under the floorboards! You are giving me such *thrills*!"

"The garden not the floorboards!" tutted Barnabus.

"Same difference!" cooed Morgan.

"Tell me" said Alf, "Is there a gentleman with the good fortune to be Mr Lefarke?"

"Not at *present* my dear!" cooed Morgan le Fake, patting Alf's hand, "The situation is *vacant*!"

Jake and Robin both spluttered and choked on their drinks.

Flipper blew a kiss to Alf.

Finn began to wonder if Flipper was enjoying his new identity a bit *too* much.

A set of Young Farmers came in fresh from their local meeting and Finn turned his back on the 'nonsense table', as he had now labelled it, and joined in their discussion about the price of sheep while serving them all down to earth legend free pints of the local craft brew.

Then the Little Wychwell silver band appeared after their practice.

Finn was now too busy to wonder what was happening upstairs, downstairs or anywhere else until closing time. He barely noticed Morgan le Fake leaving with Barnabus or Jake and Robin explaining to Alf that he very urgently needed his eyes testing.

Meanwhile the ceaseless round of singing, pause, cello, pause, both together, pause continued upstairs. From time to time Finn wondered if Stinker was *OK* but he was now so busy that any worry changed to resentment "It's *his* pub, why isn't he down here helping me when he can hear how busy it is from up there?"

By two a.m. Finn had thrown the last Young Farmer out and tidied and cleaned the bar and finished the glass washing, all these tasks were accompanied by continued streams of noise from upstairs. The noises above were much more noticeable once the customers had left as their conversation masked them slightly with a loud blur of Oxfordshire burr.

Finn felt very happy at the thought of a peaceful night's sleep in the Studio at the Old Vicarage. Elodea had left him both a drink and a snack, so he enjoyed theses, set the alarms and tucked himself up comfortably in bed.

Five minutes after Finn fell asleep Flipper, this time dressed much more suitably in a black tracksuit, black trainers and a black balaclava, materialised outside the studio door, switched off the alarms from outside, came in through the door with his newly cut key and woke Finn up again.

"*No!*" said Finn, feeling really angry, "This is *too much*! I bet you knew perfectly well I had only just gone to sleep!"

"May have estimated the likelihood of that, yes!" said Flipper.

"Just a minute!" said Finn, "I *know* I put the alarms on this time! Did you switch them off from *outside*?"

"Obviously!" said Flipper.

"So you did that *before* at the Wyching Well! I *hadn't* forgotten to set them at all!" grumped Finn.

"I *might* have!" said Flipper, "While I am confessing to that I also might have used a very powerful magnet to draw the bolt back from outside the back door of the Wyching Well."

Finn snorted, "What sort of *pathetic excuse* for a colleague and friend are you? Torturing me with thinking I had been so careless about security!" he said, "What's more that means that it's really your fault that Nimuë got in! I suppose you didn't think to put the bolt back on when you left!"

"No but you didn't bother to do it either and it was your responsibility!" protested Flipper "You know I have a twisted sense of humour and should have expected nothing else. The smell of stout on your breath was so strong I couldn't resist the temptation to remind you of the dangers of imbibing while on duty! Let me also tell you that while you have been lolling around chatting to people in a bar I was *working*! I am *worn out*! I don't know how full time drag queens cope, just wearing the clothes is so enervating! Even just the *heels*, they *kill* your feet and as for the corsets and stockings, *words fail me*! However due to my efforts I have information! I tracked one of your Young Farmers after he left. The very tall one."

"Not drink on duty? How many Gin and Tonics did you knock back while 'working' this evening?" demanded Finn, "The very tall guy is Lance Boswell. Only just come back from a gap year abroad. Charming Little Wychwell farming family who have been resident here since before the Norman Conquest. They have a huge farm. Very well off. Benevolent Pillars of the Village," said Finn.

"Hmm! Whatever his family are like we need to be *more than a little suspicious* about Lance. Where do you think he went when he left the Wyching Well?" asked Flipper.

"Home to bed or else fell over on the pavement and is sleeping where he fell, given how much alcohol he had drunk!" replied Finn.

"No, no, Young Farmers have *very* strong livers, they are not only usually large, very fit and muscular but also Young. We used to have livers like that when *we* were Young." said Flipper.

"I am still Young, Grandad! Where *did* he go then?" asked Finn.

"To the *White House*" replied Flipper.

"To the White House?" said Finn.

"Yes, not just *to* the White House but *Into* The White House" said Flipper.

"*Into* the White House?" exclaimed Finn.

"Yep, had key, opened door, went in. Shortly after that he came out. Locked door. Then went home" replied Flipper.

"Well maybe he is just checking on their post for them and making sure no one has broken in?" suggested Finn.

"Hmmm!" replied Flipper, "I'll tell you something else interesting about our friend Lance."

"What?" demanded Finn.

"As you know he has just come home from his gap year but what you don't know is that he was on the same flight to Heathrow as Stinker's little lover Nimuë. They are friends on Facebook too!" said Flipper.

Finn groaned, "Please don't tell me he sings, composes music or plays the cello or any other musical instrument!"

"Not as far as I *know*" Flipper replied, "But guess what his first name is!"

"Lance, obviously!" said Finn, sarcastically.

"No, no, that's an abbreviation, it's *Lancelot*!" replied Flipper, laughing.

"And I suppose *Lance's* girlfriend is called *Guinevere* and she is already married to someone called Arthur?" said Finn.

"Not as yet but he doesn't have a girlfriend currently so there is still time" replied Flipper.

"So is Nimuë definitely a *suspect* now?" asked Finn.

"Anyone that odd who is also a druggie and appears apparently spontaneously in such a strange way at precisely this time is *suspicious*" replied Flipper "But I don't think she is, as yet, *officially* categorised as a *suspect*."

"So it's all still wide open?" asked Finn.

"Pretty much" said Flipper.

"But if she *is* a suspect then why is she playing around with Stinker? He isn't the criminal type and it must be distracting her from whatever she is supposed to be doing here!" said Finn.

"Isn't that as clear as day?" asked Flipper.

"No!" said Finn.

"Stinker knows who she is of course!" said Flipper, "So she is using him as a cover *and* stopping him being suspicious about what she is doing in the village all at one and the same time!"

"Ok, Sherlock!" said Finn, "I agree, I am being dopey tonight! A few days in this pastoral idyll and I am this brain dead!"

"I wouldn't worry about that!" replied Flipper, "You were already brain dead compared to a genius like me!"

Finn glared at him.

"So will the expert polymath *Morgan le Fake* be calling into the Wyching Well *tomorrow*?" asked Finn.

"You never know! She *might* pop in to have a little flirt with Old Alf again!" said Flipper.

Finn threw a pillow at Flipper, "Do you *have* to?" Finn asked.

"If you keep on just playing around being a barman while you are here then this means that *I* have to continue to take on *all* the stress and the burden of *the investigation* by myself!" said Flipper.

Finn threw another pillow at him but Flipper nimbly caught it.

"Well, I'm off" said Flipper, throwing the pillow back at Finn, "You will need this one for your sweet dreams of little honey tongued red headed lassies! Don't forget to re-set the alarms!"

Finn chucked the pillow at Flipper's retreating back but the door had already closed behind him. The pillow hit the door and slid to the floor with a soft, unsatisfying and barely audible thud.

Finn stumped out of bed and across the room to retrieve both pillows, making complaining noises to himself. He reset all the alarms.

"And what's *more,* what's *even more*, is that it's back to work on the bar tomorrow! Musicians upstairs making terrible noises, customers, Flipper prancing around in petticoats and high heels, I used to *like* the Wyching Well, but that cute, ancient, traditional sleepy pub is becoming a place to which I am now pos-i-tive-ly averse. I don't suppose I will be able to get back to sleep for hours and hours now after Flipper waking me up so soon after I dozed off! Why is it called Wyching! I know Wych means white but why not call it the Wych Well not the Wyching Well? Wych, Witch, Magic, Arthurian legends" Finn moaned to himself, "This whole mission is getting creepier and creepier and I don't care if that is superstitious nonsense! Plus the previous Landlord *really* drowning in the well! Didn't want to tell Stinker in case it upset *him.* No one cares if it upsets poor Finn! No one worries about the poor innocent barman having nightmares!"

But despite his conviction of approaching insomnia as soon as he lay back down Finn fell fast asleep and smiled in his dreams.

Chapter Five

The following day Finn decided he had better get to the Wyching Well well before opening time again to get things organised and running properly. Stinker was, after all, unknowingly assisting in Finn's work and Finn did not want him to have a financial disaster as a result even if this slowed the progress of Finn's other surveillance activities.

Finn arrived at the Wyching Well at ten thirty a.m. As he expected Stinker was not getting ready for opening, there was no sign of him having been downstairs since Finn left yesterday and the composing session was continuing upstairs.

Finn sorted out the bar and cleaned the glasses and the floors.

At ten to twelve there was a crashing sound as Stinker slipped and fell down the stairs and tumbled out through the bottom door into the bar.

Finn picked him up from the floor and dusted him down.

The grey tinge in Stinker's face had increased, his eyes were bloodshot, his body was trembling.

"I say, old boy!" said Finn, "You *have* to stop this! Are you trying to *kill* yourself? You *can't* carry on with this sleep free lifestyle! Is Nimuë asleep?"

"No, she said I *could* come down and open up the bar but the customers will be *fine* alone, she was sure they would be *very* honest about paying so I am to go straight back upstairs once the front door is unlocked for them" replied Stinker.

"Have you been sidestream smoking her wacky baccy again or has she given you some dodgy pills?" demanded Finn, "You know perfectly well that the Little Wychwellers are not inclined to exercise pity on a business owner who vanishes and leaves the bar open for them."

"Oh dear! Do you think they took *much* for free the last time there was no one in the bar?" faltered Stinker.

"*Much*? I think it's a wonder you still have *any* stock! You need to do some re-ordering, we need more beer for a start off!" said Finn.

"Wholesaler phone number is pinned on the wall at the back of the bar, *you* can order some!" said Stinker.

"What? I get to do the stock orders now *too*, just so you can go and compose for Nimuë?" asked Finn, making himself sound very cross, as he felt that he had to try to rescue Stinker from Nimuë somehow, "I said I'd do the *evenings* for a fortnight, I didn't say I'd do *absolutely everything* for a fortnight!"

"But I *can't* leave this composition! If you were not here I would just have to close the place until we had finished composing and that could be weeks or even months! You have no idea how *seminal* this piece will be! Nimuë is a genius, an absolute *genius*! So far past me in compositional brilliance that I must *fade* and she *must* increase! I must lose all my powers so that I can strengthen hers! This symphony will be the most remarkable piece of music ever composed!"

Finn shivered involuntarily as he heard Stinker say 'I must lose all my powers so that I can strengthen hers', even though he told himself that there could not really be some strange conjunction happening between the past and the present in this place, 'even a hard headed person like me can see that' he thought. Then Finn reminded himself firmly that the Arthurian legends were just that, they were *legends* and the spirits in them only *fictional* spirits. 'Even so' Finn said to himself, 'something is still very, very odd. Could I be causing Stinker's strange language and behaviour through *auto*-suggestion due to my own stupid superstitious thoughts? Or is Nimuë feeding this Arthurian-style gibberish into Stinker's mind? She must know all the legends really well as her Father is an Arthurian expert, I expect she was brought up on them for her bed time stories!'

Aloud Finn said "*Complete nonsense*! Nimuë *has* been feeding you something weird and illegal hasn't she? She *must* have done compositional studies at Oxford, if she wants to compose something she can *write it all up herself*! You will go bankrupt if you close for weeks, you still have to cover all the expenses and there are no more lockdown allowances! Plus if you carry on not sleeping or eating like this you are going to be in hospital not composing on her behalf! When did you last eat anything?"

"Two days ago? Maybe? Nimuë had a big meal at two a.m. but I was too much in flow to interrupt for eating" said Stinker, pathetically.

Finn banged his own head symbolically on the wooden top of the bar.

"Did Nimuë have a lovely sleep while you rewrote all your manuscript scribbles up in neat form again?" asked Finn.

"Yes, actually, yes, she *did*! I was too excited about the music to rest! I'm past sleep! I cannot sleep ever again till she has finished this *pivotal* work!" replied Stinker.

"I'm sure you can risk *one black coffee*!" said Finn, coaxingly, "If you are primed up with caffeine you will be able to concentrate better!"

"*Maybe*" Stinker was weakening, "Just *one* coffee!"

Finn made a coffee, furtively removed three sleeping pills from his rucksack and popped them into it. 'It's *essential* for Stinker's *health*' Finn told himself.

Stinker sat at a table in bar, took the cup, sipped at it tentatively, drank about half of it in one draft and shortly afterwards slumped over on the table, dropping the cup which smashed on the floor.

"Hmmm!" said Finn, "Slightly strong reaction! Maybe three pills was one too many but Stinker is tall and hefty enough, he'll be *fine*!"

Finn picked Stinker up, dragged him unceremoniously across the room, laid him out neatly on a bench and tucked him in with a tablecloth he found behind the bar. He swept up the remains of the cup.

Then Finn shut the door to the stairs, unlocked the main door, let the waiting customers in and served them all.

Soon after that there was the sound of small feet galloping down wooden stairs and Nimuë burst in through the bottom door. She looked furious.

"Where *is* he?" she asked Finn, who decided that completely ignoring the question was the safest response.

Nlmuë looked around. She spotted Stinker tucked up on the bench on the far side of the bar.

She saw the customers.

She stopped and thought for a few moments and then realised she could do nothing with a set of the villagers looking at her with their mouths open.

Hopelessly stymied and frustrated from taking her prey back up the stairs Nlmuë then stamped her foot very hard on the floor and went back upstairs herself.

"More than one way of killing a pig!" said Finn to himself, feeling pleased.

"Is *that* Stinker's girlfriend?" Robin asked Jake, "I can see why he's a bit worn out after a night or two with *her*! No wonder he's gone and fallen asleep on the bench! I wish she was *my* girlfriend! Some women look *so* beautiful when they are angry, don't they?"

"I told you she was a looker!" said Jake, "Don't you *remember* her from before?"

"I can't say as I do!" said Robin, "But I'll take your word for it!"

From above came the sound of someone repeatedly opening and then slamming the door to Stinker's bedroom.

Finn decided the door was strong enough to take this violence and Stinker slept on completely unawares.

The sounds upstairs then changed to something that was suggestive of cups being thrown against a wall and smashing.

"Dear me, she's got a bit of a temper on her, hasn't she?" said Jake, "I love a woman with spirit! My wife once chased me right up on to the roof of our house while she ran round the garden waving a carving knife one day when I had annoyed her! Can't even remember what it was I did now!"

"Came in drunk I expect. Same as always!" said Robin.

"Entirely possible!" said Jake, "I used to get locked out of the house so I had to sleep in the garden shed nearly every Saturday night when I was younger."

The noises above changed to sudden silence.

'I hope she's not cutting the strings on his cello' Finn thought to himself.

A few minutes later a strong and unmistakeable smell of skunk being smoked filled the bar.

Finn hastened across and closed the door at the bottom of the stairs again.

'That won't stop it wafting in though' Finn thought 'Well, if the police *should* call in I shall deny All Knowledge and send them up to the flat upstairs. Would serve her right to get arrested, she might not realise that while skunk is not much of a big deal in London it's a much more heinous and exciting crime for the local police. But we can't have her getting the Wyching Well labelled as a drugs den. She will be OK if she gets arrested, Mummy and Daddy will get her out again double quick."

The smell slowly faded. 'NImuë *must* be exhausted too' thought Finn, hopefully, 'I expect she is taking the opportunity for a nap herself so she can torture Stinker all night and most of tomorrow'.

Finn heard the sound of an advancing tractor and saw Lance going slowly past the open door on a huge tractor with an equally huge trailer. Lance stopped just outside the Wyching Well.

"I hope he isn't going to leave that thing there and come in for a drink' thought Finn, 'it must be blocking the road, we will not be popular!'

Lance got out, went round the back of the tractor, apparently to fiddle around with the trailer bar connections, came back and climbed back into the cab. The tractor moved off again.

What neither Finn or any other witnesses had seen was NImuë squeezing feet first out of the very small upstairs window of the Wyching Well, being caught neatly by Lance and then being chucked up into his trailer out of sight.

All seemed calm and peaceful in the bar, only a few slow drinking customers in, so Finn was not run off his feet. Finn made himself a coffee and ate a bag of crisps, he felt relaxed and pleased with the world in general. Then he felt far less pleased as he saw Morgan le Fake mincing past the window.

"Oh no! *Not again!*" Finn said to himself "Lord protect me from my friends, I can take care of my enemies![17]"

But Flipper did not enter the bar.

About ten minutes later there was the loud retort of a gun being fired not very far away. Then several more shots.

No one in the bar was at all bothered.

"Either shooting clay pigeons or real ones I guess" explained Jake "Annual Little Wychwell Clay Pigeon Shooting Championships are on soon, you'll enjoy those young man, quite a show of shooting skills! Of course in my Father's young days it was Pigeon Shooting Championships, the most pigeons bagged in two hours anywhere within the parish boundaries, but then people went soft about killing things being cruel and whatnot and so it's only Clay Pigeons that get shot now."

"Ah" said Finn, trying not to worry too much about the conjunction of the non-appearance of Flipper and the sound of gun fire. It was true that gun fire happened frequently at any time of day or night, in Little Wychwell, poachers, gamekeepers, pheasant shooting parties, farmers protecting crops or animals, rabbit shooting parties. It was a wonder there was not an annual shooting competition *inside* the Wyching Well he mused to himself.

As if he had overheard Finn's thought's Robin spoke, "There used to be a shooting competition *right here. Inside* this bar. Yes, you may well look *surprised!* It got stopped on Health and Safety grounds about forty years

---

[17] Voltaire

ago, nobody is allowed *any fun* these days" Robin paused to sigh, wipe his mouth, and banged his glass on the table for Finn to get him another pint.

"Surely the bar isn't big enough?" asked Finn.

While Finn drew the pint Robin continued "Wait and I'll explain! It all began with a bet between two of the local nobility about who could be the first to shoot all the pips off a five of clubs at some distance or other, I forget the distance now. Then this became an *annual* shooting the pips off the playing card competition, open to all comers. By the time I can remember it happening when I was a little lad the competition had been moved to the Wyching Well. The challenge was who could fire out through the door and shoot all the pips off a five of clubs if it was fastened on that big ash tree out there and if two people or more managed *that* they added another five of clubs and another until there was only one person left in."

"I suppose the back garden fence wasn't there then?" asked Finn.

"No, no, not through the *back* door!" said Robin, waving his arms in appropriate directions as he continued, "The *front* door, firing across the street to hit a playing card pinned on *that* ash tree out *there*! Competitors had to be standing at a point on the floor that was *this* side of *that* beam in the ceiling otherwise some folk used to try *leaning out* of the front door for an *advantage*, see! Some folk were better at leaning than others."

"*Ah*" said Finn, feeling this was a safely innocuous noise to make.

"It was *perfectly* safe! We had stewards in the road *each side* to make sure no one crossed in front of the shots and got hurt, but Health and Safety is *unstoppable* these days" Robin continued "And that's why it never happens anymore!"

"Ideological soundness *gone mad*" replied Finn cheerfully and untruthfully, thinking that Health and Safety had a very sound point about people firing guns from inside a building across a road into a tree at some distance away.

"My old Grandad won the cup *four times*" said Robin, "Very proud of it he was."

"He must have been a very good shot" said Finn, politely.

"Yes, *wonderful*, always used to say he could shoot anything within fifty yards, no matter what speed it was travelling at" said Robin, "Pheasants, pigeons, rabbits, hares, deer, we were never short of food in our house when I was a boy!"

"Never" said Jake "Same in our house! All that free food running about! Then we used to pick all kinds of wild berries and mushrooms and scrump apples and the farmhands used to get free milk and cheese and eggs. Those were the days! But these days half the folk wouldn't know what their food *was* if it wasn't covered with plastic with a label on it from the supermarket or in a takeaway box!"

They both sighed.

Finn was not really listening any more. He was now *very* anxious about Flipper especially as he kept hearing *more* gun shots. He went to the front door, as if for air, so he could have a quick look up and down the street.

The street was completely empty.

Another hour passed slowly away and at last Morgan le Fake tittuped into the bar on the arm of Old Alf. Finn gave a sigh of relief. Flipper had clearly just been out making a social call but Finn hoped it was a useful social call to gather information and not Flipper *amusing himself*.

"Oooh my lovie!" Morgan purred to Finn, after tottering over to the bar on his ten inch heels, "What an afternoon I have been having! Alf has been teaching me how to *shoot* at the target he has in his back garden! I finally managed *to fire in the right direction* and after I eventually succeeded in *hitting* the target, why I was so thrilled it seemed like time to *lubricate our throats*!"

Finn glared at him, Flipper really was *overdoing* this roleplay!

"You will *improve* with *practise*!" said Alf, encouragingly, "You were making *excellent* progress!"

Finn considered the situation, Flipper getting Alf to teach him how to shoot? If there was any skill Flipper did not need to improve upon it was being a crack shot. What game was Flipper playing? Then Finn remembered that Alf's garden backed on to the very much bigger garden of the Boswell's farmhouse so Flipper could do surveillance on Lance and the rest of the Boswells while playing the fool with Alf and a gun.

'I suppose Flips is going to try claiming he has been working *really hard* all afternoon again' thought Finn to himself.

Robin frowned at Jake, "Do you think we *explained* Drag Queens *properly* to Alf last time?" he said to Jake.

Jake choked on his beer while laughing and was therefore unable to reply.

"A pint of bitter and a gin and tonic!" said Alf.

"*My* round!" gurgled Morgan le Fake.

"No, no, I insist, we have a lovely time together and I never let *ladies* pay for drinks!" replied Alf.

Morgan le Fake blew Alf a kiss and fluttered his eyelashes at him.

Finn thought that being a Drag Queen had some *financial* advantages.

Robin had such a fit of laughter that he snorted beer out over the table down his nose.

"If you want to do some extra practice *any* time just pop round, if I'm out you know where I keep all the shooting stuff" said Alf to Morgan. Alf then added "Morgan here wants to be the first Drag Queen to enter the Little Wychwell Clay Pigeon Shooting Championships! She reckons it will help give *her* career a boost if she gets a mention in the local papers for this one and it will give *our* Championship a bit of much needed publicity too, we need new sponsors now the garage has turned itself into a housing estate."

"*That explains it!*" said Jake to Robin, with a sigh of relief, "He's not quite as daft as we thought!"

Morgan le Fake smiled at Alf and cooed "But I could never manage to practice without your *help!*"

Finn wished Stinker wasn't asleep as they could have both pulled 'being sick' faces at each other behind the bar. Then he remembered that Stinker had not seen Morgan le Fake and might not recognise that it was Flipper if he did. *Buffy* then, Finn said to himself, it's a shame *Buffy* isn't here!"

As if on cue he saw John and Barnabus jogging past the window as they returned home from their afternoon run. But Barnabus did not continue much further. A couple of minutes later he reappeared through the front door, his running gear soaked with dark patches of sweat, waved at Finn and swept a look round the bar.

"Ah *there* you are!" Barnabus said to Morgan le Fake, "I was running by here along the road and I noticed that your car has a flat tyre. Do you want a hand changing the wheel so you don't *ruin your frock*?"

"A *flat tyre*? And a *man* here offering to *change* it! What a *wonderful* place this village is! I must move to Little Wychwell *double quick*!" Morgan breathed the words very seductively, "So many *men* to help a *woman* in *need*!"

Morgan finished her gin and tonic then sashayed across the bar to Barnabus and they headed out of the door together.

Finn was left wondering what *Barnabus* was up to now as well as Flipper. Or maybe what both of them were up to. Finn was beginning to feel like the only person not invited to the party. Finn went over and closed the front door again. There had been no sounds from upstairs for ages now so hopefully the drug smoking was not about to start again. Finn hoped Nimuë had joined Stinker in deepest sleep rather than revengefully and silently breaking Stinker's cello or any similar act.

"Thank you, young man!" said Alf, "It was getting a bit on the chilly side."

Finn had taken the opportunity to survey the scene in the road while closing the door. There was Morgan le Fake's dashing little Vauxhall Astra, spray painted in raspberry pink with daisy transfers all over it. There were Buffy and Morgan le Fake and they were definitely genuinely changing a tyre on it. But that didn't mean they were not both up to something else too.

'Just wait till Flipper wakes me up tonight three minutes after I have gone to sleep, just *wait*!' Finn said to himself crossly, 'He has clearly not been telling me things I might have needed to know about what he was doing today. I've a good mind to booby trap the room so he gets an electric shock when he walks towards the bed!'

Half an hour later Morgan le Fake popped her head in through the door "Well toodle-oo everyone!" she simpered, "Off home before anything *else* happens to the Daisy Mobile! Just been having a long chat with the very charming Barnabus! He knows how to make changing a wheel last while you get acquainted properly! I must get on to the Estate Agents about houses in Little Wychwell, all you lovely *boys* here!"

"Bye!" said a chorus of voices.

'Thank goodness for that!' thought Finn, "One less aggravation in the near area!"

Lance appeared on his tractor outside the Wyching Well window again, now travelling in the opposite direction and this time driving a tractor with a high cherry picker cradle attached to the front. Lance stopped again with his tractor cab blocking the window, jumped out of the door on the other side of his cab and vanished from view.

"Why did he stop now do you think?" said Jake.

"I am going to guess that Lance is either having some bad problems with his hydraulics" said Robin, "Or he has got a new job changing the bulbs in the street lights!"

Everyone laughed.

Lance reappeared inside his cab and continued on his way.

There was a lull in the drinks' orders. Finn thought that perhaps he *should* pop upstairs and check on NImuë. She had been very quiet for a long time, what if she had done some violent damage to Stinker's things or even to herself, she had been so very angry.

Finn tiptoed up the stairs with extreme caution and discovered NImuë tucked into bed and apparently fast asleep.

'Good' Finn said to himself, 'otherwise if the two of them had *both* kept being so sleep deprived there was a danger I would get here tomorrow and find they had *both* gone stark raving mad. That would have been a tremendous nuisance."

Shortly after this Lance appeared in the Wyching Well with his mate Tristan, both arriving on their feet this time.

"Two pints of your best!" said Lance.

Lance looked happy and glowing. Finn recognised that look, it was the look of a man who is either in love or besotted. Finn wondered which lucky village girl had snaffled the heir to the Boswell's huge farm.

"Had a good day?" asked Finn.

"I should say he has, look at him! Looks like our bull does when he's had a day out with the beef cows!" said Tristan, "Who's the lucky girl then?"

Lance blushed, "No one!" he said, "Just been out working all day in the fresh air!"

Tristan laughed, "Is that what you *posh* people call courting? Working? You can't fool me, you just blushed! If you want to be a liar you have to give up blushing!"

Lance punched Tristan gently in the ribs, "Look at St Wulfsige's and the Royal Agricultural University talking!" he replied, "Don't *you* go round calling *me* Posh!"

"Look at the University of Cambridge Land Economy degree talking" retorted Tristan.

Tristan punched Lance gently back in the ribs and honour was satisfied.

"So you two grew up together?" Finn asked Lance and Tristan.

"No choice! If you are the same age you can't avoid it here, the village is so small" replied Tristan.

"Must have been fun though, running around all the *fields* and things" said Finn, who was hoping to find out more about Lance, if he could get the two of them reminiscing then other facts might bounce out too.

"Lots of places to play even on wet days?" Finn persisted, "All the farm sheds?"

"Yeah, lots of places!" agreed Lance.

But neither of them seemed inclined to be very conversational with him, Finn supposed they thought he was an old man since they were both in their early twenties.

Soon they were chatting to each other about which level they had reached in various computer games. Finn's enquiries were not making much progress again.

Clive Patterson, the artist who had converted the Studio at the Old Vicarage, and Frederick Heron, the local Interior Designer, came in.

"A bottle of your Cabinet Sauvignon, young Finn!" Clive said, "And two glasses!"

Finn felt his comparative age correcting itself, Clive could tell he was young, even if Lance and Tristan thought he was too old to have a conversation with them!

Finn served them and Clive went to sit at the window table with Frederick.

But the bottle of Cabinet Sauvignon and Finn's earlier questions had jogged a memory in Tristan's brain.

"Hmmm! Talking about when we were very young and played around the village" Tristan said to Lance, "Do you remember playing in the Baldock's wine cellars?"

"Course I do!" said Lance, "Great times! The best!"

"The Baldock's wine cellar?" asked Finn.

"Yes, you know, the White House, that one near the tree *you* like climbing, *Cyril's* tree!" said Tristan.

Finn reflected that it was impossible to do anything in this village without the entire set of inhabitants knowing about it.

"Oh, *that* house. Doesn't look big enough to have much of a wine cellar" Finn replied.

"Ah, but the cellar didn't go with *that* house" said Sam, "There used to be a great big Victorian pile of a house there, so the oldies say, four storeys high, twenty or thirty bedrooms with the nursery wing, servant's quarters on the top floor, ballroom, that sort of stuff and then below the ground there were cellars for food and wine and ice and things. *It* was called the White House too."

'Why did I not know about *that*?' wondered Finn, 'Briefing team slipping up again?'

"What happened to it?" asked Finn.

"Oh it burnt down, late Victorian times, very tragic, some of the family and servants burned to death but I don't remember who it was exactly that died. No one wanted to build there again for years and years. The site got a reputation as unlucky and even cursed and most definitely haunted. Then someone sensible with their feet on the ground who didn't care *what* had happened there before came in and and cleared the site up and built the White House, and a *very nice house* it is too. Can't be living with superstition holding progress back all the time!" said Lance.

"And you played there?" asked Finn, thinking that the demise of the house in the 19ᵗʰ Century explained why the Briefing team did not think it important to the current investigation.

"When it was a wet day and we got tired of our *own* barns we used to pop round there sometimes. The Baldocks liked children and always welcomed us in, all the village children popped round there from time to time because we used to get lemonade and biscuits and if we were *really* lucky they let us go down the old cellar steps in the garden and run about in the cellars. They never went down there themselves so we could do what we liked once we were down there! It was all as it had been when the house burnt down. Even a few wine bottles still there on racks. We managed to prise the cork out of one once but it smelt disgusting. Tristan here, being an idiot, risked a big slurp to try the flavour and even though he spat it straight out again he spent the *whole night* being sick!" said Lance.

"*Don't remind me!*" said Tristan, "The stupid things you do at that age! It was *vile*, I can still taste it now! It was a good place when we got to be teenagers too, we used to nip round there with our girlfriends, in over the back wall if the gate was locked, open up the trapdoor in the garden and go down out of sight of everyone! By then the Baldocks were as deaf as posts and never knew we were there!" Tristan laughed.

"So the entrance to the cellars is in the *garden*?" asked Finn.

"Well yes, the cellars were the same size as the whole ground floor of the original house and that house covered most of the garden, so the cellar entrance was inside the old house, but outside in the garden for the new one. *Huge*, the cellars go down a couple of storeys as well as the main part of the house going up four storeys!" said Lance.

"Another two pints!" said Tristan, tiring of this conversation and banging his glass down on the bar.

The computer games discussion resumed. But Finn had already found out what he needed to know.

Chapter Six

Flipper did not need to wake Finn up when he popped round to the Studio that night for Finn was sitting upright, fully dressed and waiting for Flipper to appear so he could tell him about his discoveries.

"Just *wait* till you hear *this*!" he said to Flipper.

"No, just wait till *you* hear *this*!" replied Flipper.

"We can't both wait! This is the problem with being totally off grid for communications" said Finn.

"Tell me about it!" said Flipper, in Morgan le Fake's voice "All the travelling around from home to here is driving me mad! Let alone having to wear *stockings* half the time! How do people wear *stockings all* the time!"

"Well, bags Me first for Show and Tell!" said Finn, "Before I forget the details! It's a long yarn so listen up! It was pretty tiring serving all evening, doing all the cleaning and then I had wake Stinker up, get him off his bench and stuff some food in him before I let him go back upstairs! The funny thing is the Little Wychwellers were not at all freaked out by the sight of the Landlord spending the whole evening sleeping under a tablecloth on one of the few benches, even though it meant that three *more* people had to stand up all evening."

 "Rural dwellers are very adaptable folk!" said Flipper.

"Well, no, not quite. I realised none of them even seemed to have noticed that Stinker was asleep there so I casually mentioned to one of the regulars that Stinker seemed to be sleeping through *all* the work and leaving it all to *me* and he said *that was Old Stinker all over*! He said that if Stinker had a fit of musical inspiration and stayed up all night composing his own pieces he quite often took a nap on that bench all evening. They didn't mind at all as they all helped themselves to drinks, so many that they even sometimes paid for a few of them just in case Stinker went bankrupt otherwise. He said they called it a 'Free Freehouse Day'."

"How *does* he manage to survive financially?" asked Flipper.

"I suppose he gets a few royalty payments for his composing but I doubt that adds up to much. I guess he must have inherited a fair bit, even as a younger son and 'spare'! Also Stinker's lifestyle is very frugal so provided the takings cover the costs of things like the rates and repairs I don't think he worries much. I keep hoping he will regain a bit of sanity with respect to NImuë though, I tried to drive some into his head before I let him go back upstairs this evening but I got the definite impression that he was not listening to *any* of my very sound advice" replied Finn.

"*No hope*!" said Flipper, "He's a *musician* and, even worse, he's a *composer*! Not an ounce of sense can fit into the brain of anyone so afflicted! Look up the life stories of Famous Composers and you will see the problem. Stinker and NImuë will still be caterwauling away when you get there tomorrow, or rather when you get there *today*. Look at the time! It's nearly three a.m. and I have to cycle back to Oxford. Stop speculating about Stinker and get on with your actual information if you have any. I haven't got time for gossip!"

So Finn told Flipper about the cellars.

"Ah, *that's* what geophys found then!" said Flipper, "They thought they were just the foundations of the old house."

"You *knew* about the old house that burnt down?" demanded Finn.

"Page two hundred and five of the briefing notes, footnote five, previous large structure on the site, probably a house, risk of pieces of old foundations as trip hazards anywhere in the gardens! I checked the geophys appendix to find out why there were old foundations. I suppose you dashed straight past that footnote because you have never fallen over old foundations in gardens in the dark. If you had ever done so you would prick up your ears and pay attention to *any* such suggestion, I gouged a huge hole in my leg tripping over a fragment of old wall once, blood everywhere let alone the shock of hitting the ground suddenly and unexpectedly and wondering if I had been shot!" replied Flipper, "*Cellars* though! *Operational* ones fit for use! That is *something else*! I suppose one or both of us need to go and have a recce down there?"

"S'pose" said Finn cautiously, "But we need to get better intelligence about what we are recce-ing first. If the cellars are as big as Lance claims we need a map or something. I don't want to finish my days dying in a cellar in Little Wychwell because I can't find the way out. There must be plans of the original house somewhere? Maybe they are filling the cellars up with oil so when the price rises they can resell it all or use it all or do whatever people do with hoarded stuff these days? Then we drop in through a trapdoor and drown in oil. When I was younger I would have just bounced straight in, but now I am older I have become less rash!"

"Could fix the entire set of mysteries about that house with one match if they are full of oil *and* dispose of the oil as well!" said Flipper, "At least it might explain where they are *putting* all the oil!""

"But why would you fill cellars that also run right under the current house with oil? Apart from the danger of fire why would anyone keep twenty five years supply of heating oil under their garden?" asked Finn.

"Why would anyone buy 10 freezers and fill them all with hoarded food they will never eat because there was a rumour that that sort of food was in short supply?" asked Flipper.

"S'pose!" said Finn.

They thought for a few moments but nothing came to either of their minds.

"And *your* news?" asked Finn.

"Fits in rather well with yours, *as it happens*! Also makes the idea that it's just an oil storage depot very unlikely" replied Flipper.

"Oh no, hold on, hold on! *Before* your news..." said Finn, "What did you need to chat about to Buffy so urgently that you let one of your own tyres down to lure him into your private lair?"

"Why ever would I have let down *my own* tyre?" asked Flipper, "Plus you can't call the cute little Daisy Mobile my *lair*!"

"I can't believe you have named that pile of overpainted rust 'the Daisy Mobile'. You are sliding down the Hill of Sanity alongside Stinker! It's *not* cute, it's a fossil fuel guzzling ancient car! As to *why* you would have punctured your own tyre" replied Finn, "that is what *I* would like to know! You arrived at the Wyching Well at just the right time for Buffy to be coming back from his run soon afterwards and so you let your own tyre down by sticking a spike of some sort into it just before you came in so that he would come in to tell you and you could both go and change the tyre. This is perfectly clear to me. Do not try to argue out of it. It would have served you right if you *had* had to change the tyre *by yourself* much later while wearing that completely ridiculous outfit!"

"No chance of *that*!" said Flipper, "Lots of *men* in the pub! Always ready to help a *girl* in distress!"

"Not when she's a *fake* girl!" said Finn.

"Good thing that fake girls can change tyres themselves in that case, even if they are wearing a frilly dress" returned Flipper, "But I don't see why you think *I* punctured the tyre. Anyone can get a flat in this road! All the nails and things falling off agricultural machinery and lying around on the ground in this village."

"Agricultural machinery is not fastened together with *nails*, I presume you mean *bolts*" replied Finn.

"No, no, this was *definitely* a nail for we *found* it *in the tyre*. Must have fallen out of someone's tool box or maybe a home-made wooden trailer or whatever. Could have come from *anywhere*!" answered Flipper, but his lips quivered at the edges as he tried not to laugh.

"The nail came *from your own pocket*, don't try telling me otherwise! *So,* what *were* you chatting about with Buffy that you needed to get him out of earshot first?" demanded Finn.

"Hmmm!" said Flipper, "Let me *try to remember*. It was Buffy's usual non-stop and mainly meaningless stream of chat, I think. Rugby, the current state of UK rowing, erm…"

"And *what else*?" demanded Finn.

"Ah, yes, now I recollect, after some vaguely interesting sports chitchat he started telling me about *the other people who live in his road*.

Unbelievably boring set of really well-behaved people who mostly have children or visiting grandchildren and if not children or grandchildren then dogs, cats, pet carp in the fishpond et al, the full tick box list for desirable life. It all sounded *utterly dire!*" said Flipper, "It was fortunate that it did not take very long to change the tyre and that Buffy needed to go home to get changed out of his disgustingly sweat covered running gear or I would have nodded off!"

"OK, OK, I give up *for now*! I will find out which information you were actually getting out of Buffy in the end! Or which secrets you were exchanging with each other out of my hearing range! *Your* news then!" said Finn.

"What a *deeply suspicious mind* you have! You could take up a career as *some kind of investigator!*" said Flipper, "Ah, *my news*, well, really, it's so long since I came in and you have been monopolising the entire conversation and I am not sure I can remember it now!"

They were both sitting side by side on the edge of Finn's bed. Finn batted Flipper with a pillow.

"Get on with it!" Finn said.

"I must remember to confiscate those pillows next time I pop by and you are out, I am sure Elodea did not intend them to be used as *weapons*" said Flipper, "My News! To begin with – guess who actually owns the White House. Although Briefings might have screwed up a bit on the *cellars* not being just *foundations* they have done really well on *this* one. They have been beavering away to find out who owns the White House for weeks. It has been very hard to trace since they had to work backwards through many offshore trusts, holding companies and such like. I'll give you a big clue...name a really big Global Corporation of the most dubious nature possible. Owns large media companies as well as real estate, construction firms, travel companies, fashion houses, shares in fossil fuel production and is one of the worst climate change emitters on the Planet but the CEOs have managed to retain a cuddly Ma and Pop image."

"Not Mordred Corp?" asked Finn.

"Got it in one!" said Flipper.

"Oh well!" said Finn, "That's it then! Game over! End of Project! Where am I going on assignment next?"

"No, not over at all!" replied Flipper.

"Of course it's over! Discreet communication with Cabinet Secretary, whole investigation closed! We aren't going to try going head to head with Mordred Corp, are we? Hand in fist with the Government and the Opposition and not even just in the UK, hand in fist with Governments all over the Globe! Too rich to ever be arrested! *Parvus pendetur fur, magnus abire videtur!*[18]"

"But *no!*" said Flipper, "The Boss has gone All Eco, which tells you how bad Climate Change is now! The Boss says that Mordred Corp have been destroying the Planet for long enough and if Mordred Corp can be knocked off their perch that would be a *good thing*. So there will be no upwards communications on this one. Truly hush hush in *all* directions! One of the reasons you are off grid. They must have been suspicious about who was running this one from the start."

"Off grid to stop the Cabinet Office spying? Could be! I have noticed The Boss has gone all Eco. I have a bicycle here but no car. I cycled here in the first place. I have no idea how you managed to wangle an ancient Vauxhall Astra." snorted Finn.

"It's not just to prevent the Cabinet Office listening in, remember there is high level IT ability on the criminal side. But blocking other Govt departments also stops the risk of Mordred Corp being sold any leaked information !" said Flipper, "As to the Daisy Mobile, you could hardly expect Morgan le Fake to *cycle* with her outfits! Essential for cover too as the Daisy Mobile is *so very her*! Also I am *your* emergency vehicle!"

"Fat lot of use if I have an emergency that needs a car when you are fifteen miles away! I'd do better to, er, *temporarily requisition* Frederick Heron's vintage sports car and hope it has enough petrol in the tank. He is an ultra carbon zero Interior Designer so, as one might expect, he drives a

---

[18] The petty thief is hanged, the big thief gets away

high powered 1980s Ferrari" Finn laughed and continued, "So, what other news bear you hither by mouth to the Pre Online Communications Stone Age?" asked Finn.

"The Boss is *right* about Eco, you do *know* that don't you?" pleaded Flipper.

"Yes, the Boss is right! Things are *desperate*. I just object to *me* saving emissions while *you* pump them out from an antique Vauxhall Astra!" protested Finn.

"As I said, that car is very *in character*!" retorted Flipper "And in case you also hadn't noticed I cycled *back* here just now from Oxford! I cycle *every* time I am not Morgan le Fake!"

"Well that will be handy if we both need an emergency vehicle, two bicycles!" responded Finn.

"As you suggested, we will just have to borrow Frederick's without leave, *simples*!" said Flipper.

"Not borrow and definitely not steal! *'Requisition for emergency use'*!" corrected Finn.

"If you *prefer*" said Flipper, "Now let me make your current favourite delusional paranoia much worse. Name the Directors of Mordred Corp!" added Flipper.

"Art and Gwyn Jones!" said Finn.

"This is what they are commonly called! But if we use their *full* names instead of abbreviations" replied Flipper, "what are they *really* called?"

"I don't know" said Finn, "But I have a sinking feeling!"

"And your sinking feeling is *totally* correct! Arthur and Gwenivar are their original given names, Gwenivar being the Breton form of Guinevere" said Flipper, with a note of triumph.

"And *Mordred* Corp! This just isn't possible! This is too much fortuitous incidence! Who do we have in this case now? Arthur, Guinevere, Nimuë, Stinker who was nearly named Merlin by his Mother, Morgan le Fake,

Lancelot who has a friend called Tristan, remember one of Arthur's knights was Tristan, and *Mordred* Corp"

"How do you know that one of Arthur's knights was called Tristan. You must have *looked that up*! You have started looking your own delusions up!" said Flipper.

"You are wrong, I knew already!" said Finn, dishonestly and hoping Flipper did not look at the shelves and see a pile of books about Arthur that he had borrowed from Elodea.

"But, and more to the point, Mordred is more than just a Corp, it's a human too! Mordred Corp is named after Arthur and Gwenivar's son *Mordred*!" said Flipper.

"No, *please not*! I *will* go mad if this carries on!" said Finn, "These coincidences are too frequent! We have slipped into an alternative universe and the case is following a strange parallel to the Arthurian legends!"

"Get a grip!" said Flipper, "Talk about *me* sliding down the Hill of Sanity with Stinker! You have already beaten both of us to the bottom. None of these names are *at all* surprising. For example, NImuë and Mordred and Stinker-who-was-nearly-named-Merlin are all the same age and so King Arthur might have been in fashion in the year in which they were born."

"They are *all the same age*?" asked Finn.

"Did I not mention that before about Mordred? They were *all* music students at Oxford at the same time! Although if was due to a popular cultural fad one might ask why we and Buffy and all our other Oxford friends do not have Arthurian Names too as we are also the same age" replied Flipper, "I suppose all our parents were less swayed by Fashion!"

"You *cannot* be serious, Mordred read music with Stinker and Nimuë? Did he play the cello too?" asked Finn.

"Oh but I *am serious*" said Flipper, "Not just all music students together but Nimuë and Mordred used to go out *with each other* for nearly the whole of their time in Oxford before their break up in their final term and her *very* brief fling with Stinker, now referred to as '*when Stinker became my boyfriend'*."

"How do you know they went out together?" asked Finn.

"You have realised that if NImuë and Mordred and Stinker are all the same age then they are also the same age as us?" asked Flipper.

"Ah! So you *knew* them when we were at Oxford?" asked Finn.

"Not as *close* acquaintances, no" said Flipper, "But in case you missed this fact NImuë is a very attractive looking woman and was even more good looking when younger and less drug and alcohol raddled. She was so stunning that if a susceptible male saw her then he never forgot her. *You*, being a well behaved, serious and studious student, were probably exercising or studying or something when she went past and thus avoided seeing the available female talent. Myself, yes, I sort of noticed her about the place sometimes and since she was attached by the hip to Mordred every time then seeing her and him together has also stuck in my brain."

"Mordred wasn't at *Kings* was he?" asked Finn.

"No, no, *Coromandel!*" replied Flipper, "*With* Stinker *and* NImuë! Did I not say that?"

"NImuë and Mordred are both from monied backgrounds but Stinker's very posh too so with reading the same subject I suppose they would have all been in the same coterie" said Finn, "Of course Stinker's been bumped a bit in the social hierarchy these days now his brother has inherited the estate and he is definitely 'spare'. While I am rudely labelling people as posh and over privileged that applies to *you* too!"

"The Dead have no social status or inheritance"[19] intoned Flipper solemnly, "And" he added, brightening up, "one of the *best* bits about being Dead I not having to be Posh any more, I will admit that! No responsibility, no ancestors to live up to, no having to remember that one must not besmirch the family reputation, no really boring events you *have* to attend as a matter of duty, no shoots, no hunts, no balls, no anything!

---

[19] All that Glisters is not Silver

Only the Upper Class can sit in one spot and do almost nothing for a whole afternoon or evening while wearing such uncomfortable clothes it makes Morgan le Fake's outfits look like casual wear and yet *never* look bored or get out of temper. Only the Upper Class can get up before at five a.m. to dress correctly for a hunt or shoot, get cold and wet, pay extra to bring the pheasants they shot themselves back home and smile about it. They are disgusting too, one can only hope the servants dispose of them rather than hanging them for months just to serve something full of bits of shot. Yet all the time the Upper Class maintain a polite front and say it was *tremendous fun.* You lot are not trained properly! This is why you all whine all the time!" Flipper laughed.

"What?" said Finn.

"So" continued Flipper, "This is why those of us who are trained properly all develop cynical attitudes to the Arthurian legends and all other chivalric tales!"

"Eh?" said Finn.

"Because our permanent occupation of being bored and immobile yet looking interested and polite began with them. First when the Romantic concept of Chivalry was invented in medieval times and then even more so when the Victorians rediscovered the Idea of Rules and Chivalry and made Upper Class Restrictive Behaviour Rules at least four times worse."

"I had never realised the level of your suffering before" said Finn, sarcastically, "I tell you what, why don't you start a Pod Cast or get a series on Spotify or something so you can fully bemoan the tragic life of the very rich and privileged."

Flipper glared at him and said, "So, let me return to disillusioning you about any recent events being preordained due to some long shadow stretching forth from ancient times and pointing to Little Wychwell. Firstly the Arthurian Legends have no basis in reality that has ever been proven. Secondly, even if we assume they *are* based on reality, there is no strange synchronicity happening here. Mordred and NImuë would clearly have been attracted to each other at Oxford by the association between their own names, just as the same thing would have happened to Arthur and

Gwenivar when they met long before that. Arthur and Gwenivar would have been very likely to choose something Arthurian for their own child because of their own names and that explains the name Mordred. NImuë happened to have a Father who studied Arthurian legend which is how she got her name. Plus, as I said before, there may have been something Arthurian in popular culture in the year of all our births on top of that. It probably a wonder that the two of us are not called Belvedere and Percival. Tristan is a popular name for someone of Tristan's age, probably connected to another cultural reference as no one except you even remembers that he was one of Arthur's Knights, and Lancelot just *happens* to be called Lancelot! He is very likely named after one of his relatives!"

Flipper stopped for breath and then resumed, "I will continue through this debunking, *I called myself* Morgan le Fake just as a *wind up* because it matched in with Nimuë and Stinker-who-was-nearly-called-Merlin. There is *nothing* spooky about that! Although another little-known Knight of King Arthur was Sir Finisterre so I suppose he could have been called Finn for short and perhaps that should be of some concern...."

Flipper broke off as Finn clouted him with a pillow again, *"You made that last bit up!"* Finn said, "I will admit I read up on *all* the names of people who feature in the Arthurian legends in case any more of them popped up in the Wyching Well and that is how I knew that Tristan was one of the Knights! But it is also how I know that there was *no Sir Finisterre*. You just got that name from a now removed label for an area in the Shipping Forecast. Plus Finn isn't even my *real* name as you know perfectly well!"

"Learning all the names of the people in the Arthurian Legends? What next?" said Flipper, "You are not even at the bottom of the Hill of Sanity - you have slid right off the end of it into a very deep crevasse! Are you going to keep wasting time by hitting me with pillows so that we both finish up as sleep deprived as Stinker or would you like to hear the rest of my news *without* further diversions?"

"I don't *absolutely* have to get up till about eleven a.m., having a job as a stand in Landlord is great from that point of view, hours of time for sleeping left" said Finn, "But *pray continue.*"

"Right, *where was I*?" said Flipper, "Perhaps I'll leave the rest of this story for tomorrow. I am getting tired of having to transmit so much information!"

"*No you don't*" said Finn, "Continuer! L'ouïe de l'oie de Louis a ouï. — Ah oui ? Et qu'a ouï l'ouïe de l'oie de Louis ? — Elle a ouï ce que toute oie oit... — Et qu'oit toute oie ? — Toute oie oit, quand mon chien aboie, le soir au fond des bois, toute oie oit : ouah ! ouah !, qu'elle oit, l'oie !"[20]

Flipper frowned, "How am I meant to continue with *anything* sensible if you spout nonsense phrases in French? Is this what happens when you are sent out off grid and free from surveillance? If so it's time they put you back on so I don't have to endure this outbreak of continuous babbling of rubbish that has clearly been suppressed over years of only saying sensible things! Just keep ta bouche fermée and I will finish what I have to say!"

Finn put his finger on his own lips and Flipper began again.

Flipper continued "I have told you that Mordred and Nlmuë were girlfriend and boyfriend for a lot of their Oxford careers, but I have not told you some more *really important* news. Wait for this bit! The White House was not the *only* Little Wychwell house that is owned by Mordred Corp via a mysterious chain of other shadowy companies. When they bought *that* house they also bought one in the same road as Buffy and Angel's house!"

"Ah! The nail in the tyre makes sense at last!" said Finn.

"Think of the *suffering* I had to undergo to get any facts about the inhabitants of *that* house! I endured Buffy telling me gossip and trite facts about *every other* family in the road first, plus odd bits of probably untrue Local History that he had embroidered with spurious details. But I finally discovered that the house owned by Mordred Corp in Buffy's road is lived in by a certain Phineas Floyd, an elderly man who is still shielding due to the continuing risk of Covid because he is in poor health. You will rejoice

---

[20]A French Trompe d'oreille

to hear that the shielding has been effective as he has so far managed not to catch it!" said Flipper.

"*That's the news*? Elderly man *doesn't* catch Covid? Hmmm! But Phineas Floyd" mused Finn, "Should be easy to find out everything about him, there can't be many people in the UK called *that*?"

"It would be easy if it was his *real* name. But what is even more amazing is that there is *no such person* as a Phineas Floyd of his age and appearance in the UK" replied Flipper, "However an unusual and difficult to disguise fact about Mordred is that he is *very small*. He is only about the same size as Nlmuë. *So is Phineas Floyd*."

"So are lots of shrunken in stature elderly frail men, and maybe he just chooses to call himself that name. He could be called Something Else Floyd. There are lots of people with the surname Floyd. Not conclusive!" said Finn.

"No, but it adds high conjectural probability to the idea that Phineas Floyd is Mordred in disguise" said Flipper, "The house of concern is Number Twenty by the way!"

"Assuming it is him does he move about to and from the White House do you think? Can we catch him in motion?" asked Finn.

"Possible" replied Flipper "But if he does go out of his house he does so without any one else like Buffy observing him do so. As you know, in Little Wychwell, a *mouse* cannot walk down the road in daylight, or even in darkness, without being seen. Therefore he must go out of his back garden and round by the fields in the dark and then in through the back wall of the White House. Even this would require caution to avoid observance as there are enough poachers, game keepers and legal night shooters and late or early dog walkers about. The lights and music go on and off at various times in the White House but that appears to be operated remotely or automatically. Just as whatever the White House is being used for could be operated completely remotely, even if we are right in assuming that Phineas Floyd is Mordred and that Mordred is behind the White House Mystery. However it seems more likely to be operated in situ as we have not detected any IT transmissions in or out of the house or garden."

"Find one fact, get another fifty two mysteries!" said Finn.

"We progress, we *progress*!" said Flipper, in a soothing tone, "Now, we need to discuss our next moves in the game!"

■■

Chapter Seven

By the time Flipper left it was a quarter to five a.m. and he had to hurry to cycle away before being sighted by early rising farmers and builders. Finn no longer felt like having any sleep. He looked at the time and had a good idea.

Fifteen minutes later he glided across the lawn and joined Elodea in the Kitchen of the Old Vicarage where she was putting the kettle on with her back to the door. Elodea jumped when Finn tapped her on the shoulder and then smiled at him.

"It's OK, it's only me! Shhhhh though!" Finn said to her "I am *not here*! Mustn't upset *John*! I can't sleep so I thought some coffee might help me wake up instead!"

"I don't think *caffeine* will help with *sleep*. Although I always have a cup of coffee before bed myself and I have to say I don't *think* it affects my ability to go to sleep, but then I never sleep very well whatever I do" Elodea replied, "I'm just boiling the kettle for a brew now, have a stool!"

She pushed a kitchen stool towards him with one foot while putting ground coffee into a percolator.

"Boiled egg?" she said to him, "I always find them very restorative and you looked tired, I hope it's not the bed!"

"Rather! I love boiled eggs!" Finn replied, "No, no, the bed is *very* comfortable! *Most* grateful, thank you enormously!"

"Hard or soft?" she asked.

"Don't mind in the slightest!" said Finn, "Either or both!"

Elodea put some eggs into cold water and put it on the stove to come up to the boil.

"So, how is life in the Studio going? Satisfactory?" she asked.

"Absolutely *super*!" replied Finn.

Finn considered what Elodea was wearing. It looked like a sweatshirt and a pair of jeans to him, had she run out of her evening wear? Or was it a designer sweatshirt and jeans as a form of formal wear? He felt he had to know.

"Have you run out of evening dresses?" he asked her.

"No, no!" she said, "I will explain!"

But instead of explaining she looked at the now bubbling pan and began to count "and one and two and three and ....."

To Finn's surprise Tony then materialised in the kitchen not only did he achieve this so silently that even Finn was impressed but Finn had thought Tony was still on remand in prison. Finn tried to think how to comment on Tony's release without saying the wrong thing by mistake but failed. He decided saying nothing was the safest option.

Tony looked at his Mama who was still counting.

"Lost the kitchen timer *again*?" Tony said, "why don't you use your *phone* to time things?"

"Twenty six because it uses energy unnecessarily thirty one..." replied Elodea and continued to count.

Tony sighed, "Even *I* think that's going a bit far, Mama, it can't be more than a tiny amount of battery power" he said, "But you *could* be right! It wears the battery down so it needs replacing sooner I suppose and that means using more lithium."

"OK, OK, I dropped my phone in a puddle yesterday while I was taking Grandson of Babe out, it's completely non-functional currently but it's drying out on top of the boiler. Don't try phoning or texting me today!" replied Elodea, "Don't mention it to Dad either, he is very grumpy about the fact I managed to get it wet *yet again*!"

The huge pile of fur and legs in the corner thumped its tail up and down with enthusiasm at the sound of his own name and then subsided.

"Ah *Finn*!" Tony said, suddenly registering Finn's presence in the kitchen, "Mama said last night that word in the village is that you are very good at climbing big trees and sitting up them?"

"*Passable*" replied Finn, cautiously.

"We could do with *all* the people we can get at present. It's getting difficult to keep enough people there to stave the devils off, people have jobs and homes and things and they can't all commit full time and then some of us got detained and most of us are still detained *inside* so we couldn't help either!" said Tony.

"Ah, yes, *the Boundary Oak*? The one between Little Wychwell and Upper Storkmorton. Protest going *well*?" asked Finn.

"*Holding them off*, but we need more people!" answered Tony.

"I'm not really allowed to do that sort of thing, you know how it is" replied Finn.

"I *suppose* not!" said Tony, sounding regretful, "Maybe you could pretend to be someone else while you were there? Or pretend to be an infiltrator and actually not be one?"

"I'll bear it in mind if I ever get a day off" answered Finn, crossing his fingers behind him as he spoke, "But I'm very, *very* glad to see you *here*!" Finn continued.

"Got out yesterday! Charges *dropped*! Not that they *had* a charge in the first place! Trying to Save the Planet is *not* a crime! I would have rather stood trial so I could have told them what I thought face to face but..."said Tony.

"One hundred and twenty, of course you wouldn't have rather have had all the strain of a trial and being stuck in prison any longer, be very thankful you are safe home" said Elodea, "one hundred and twenty five!"

"But I still think *Flic's parents* had something to do with it" said Tony, "and that's *wrong*, that's unfair on anyone *else* who gets arrested for Saving the Planet and doesn't have super rich in laws!"

"No, of course they didn't" said Elodea, "The prosecutors just decided the case could not be won, which it couldn't because there wasn't a case, one hundred and forty, one hundred and forty one."

"*Whatever* reason brought you back" said Finn, intervening hastily, "It's excellent that you *are* here. I'm not *here* by the way, I'm not allowed in the house by your Dad, I'm only allowed in the *Studio*!"

"Roger! *Noted*! Don't want to upset the Sire! I'd best be off myself!" replied Tony.

"Aren't you on an injunction *not* to climb trees now?" asked Finn.

"*And*?" replied Tony, "*Is the Planet worth having*?"

"Well, quite, absolutely!" replied Finn, in a soothing tone.

"I speak for the oak, not just for that oak, all oaks, not just for oaks but for all trees*, I speak for the trees for the trees have no tongues*[21]" said Tony, "We will have no Living Planet unless we *all* speak for all of them!"

"Quite, *quite so*!" said Finn.

"Bye Mama! Bye!" said Tony, blowing kisses at her and then he opened the door and stepped out into the beauty of the sunrise.

"Why does everyone else not get up and out early?" Tony asked himself as he breathed in gulps of fresh morning air, "If everyone saw sunrise every day, if they heard the dawn chorus and felt the dew and the rain and sleet and snow, even if only just at this magical time of day, then they would realise why the World is too precious to lose and why all the wild things matter so much!"

Tony had missed this so much for the last few weeks, he mounted his bicycle and rode away, smiling and whistling a happy tune.

---

[21] Dr. Seuss — '*I am the Lorax. I speak for the trees. I speak for the trees* for the trees *have no tongues.*' (a story of environmental disaster via avaricious felling of trees)

Back in the kitchen Elodea finally got to one hundred and eighty while buttering copious slices of toast and scooped the eggs into animal shaped egg cups.

"I am so proud of Tony!" said Elodea, "I know he has huge principles but I never realised the full extent of his courage until recently. I do hope he doesn't get arrested again though! And" she added, "the Lorax was right![22]"

"Yes, yes, *entirely* right!" replied Finn with enthusiasm, thinking that trees were indeed, most important, while also thinking that he must find out what a Lorax *was* later today.

"Don't you *love* these egg cups?" she asked Finn, as he looked rather dubiously at his very-ugly-frog egg cup, "John used to love these when *he* was small, and then *our* children and now *their* children do when *they* come round."

"Yes, *absolutely super*!" said Finn, crossing his fingers behind his back.

"To get back to what I was saying *before* I started to count!" said Elodea, as they both hit their eggs with teaspoons and scooped the tops off, "When I had the *little discussion* with John about you living in the Studio for a while, we *also* got on to the fact that John's Faculty and College are going back to having formal dinners and events again this year. So John said that perhaps I do *not* have too many formal occasion wear clothes after all and that perhaps I *can* stop wearing them all out now. John now agrees that we have plenty of room for them all in the wardrobes and buying more instead would be much worse environmentally."

"*Ah*!" said Finn, in an '*I understand*' way, thinking that must have been a really good row and feeling a little guilty about being the underlying cause of it, but also thinking that he did not have to guess who had won it.

"I suppose you knew Tony was back before he came down?" said Elodea, hopping on to another subject.

"No, no, I had no idea, but I am *delighted* to see him" Finn replied.

"*They* didn't tell you?" asked Elodea.

---

[22] The Lorax by Dr Seuss

"No, really, we are only briefed on things relevant to the case we are working on" replied Finn.

"But Tony lives here and you are in the Studio. I thought they might have warned you about dangerous and reckless criminal tree climbers in your vicinity?" asked Elodea.

"I don't think Tony would classify as a high-level criminal" smiled Finn.

"I thought at first *you* had managed to get him out. I *was* going to thank you!" said Elodea, sounding disappointed and disillusioned about Finn, "But I see it wasn't you at all since you did not even know he was back."

"No, no, I don't lie, I'm very sorry but managing anything of the sort would be *way* out of my remit, otherwise I *would* have, I *promise* you!" replied Finn.

"You don't *lie ever*?" asked Elodea, "Isn't that a little inconvenient in your work?"

"That's not lying, that's roleplay for my work!" replied Finn, "It's *morally* different!"

"Hmmm!" said Elodea, with a touch of a snort, "I suppose it *must* have been Flic's parents then!"

"I have *no idea* who got him out!" Finn replied, "I really and truly don't know! It's entirely possible that there *was* insufficient case against Tony! Or maybe somebody screwed up the custody papers or the charge or something!"

"*Money talks* as they say" replied Elodea, "And those with lots of it can always get their own way!"

"It costs a lot to bring failed prosecutions and a lot of lawyers are now refusing to prosecute Planet Defenders, I can't imagine Tony beat any of the security people up so there probably was only a very thin case and maybe they thought he was going to win!" answered Finn.

"It would be lovely to think that the Powers That Be actually *cared* about Life on Earth" said Elodea, "But I fear they only worry about *losing votes*."

"So" said Finn, changing the subject since it was getting increasingly uncomfortable, "How are Barnabus and Angel getting on? And all the children?"

By the time Finn left thirty minutes later he had managed to move Elodea on to discussing all the people who lived in Buffy's road and had amassed some more facts about Phineas Floyd and also a whole lot of information on the rest of Buffy and Angel's neighbours that he did not want to know at all, including all their voice ranges and their potential for, if not membership of, the church choir.

"I suppose *you* don't sing?" asked Elodea hopefully.

"No" Finn replied, quite untruthfully as he had a very good baritone voice, and then rather wickedly added, "But Nimuë at the Wyching Well has the voice of a *diva*, astonishing, you should ask *her*!"

"That's a good idea!" Elodea said, "Lance is back in the choir now that he has returned from his gap year abroad and *he* suggested we asked Nimuë *himself*!"

"Jolly good!" said Finn and thought to himself, 'Lance is *in* the church choir and furthermore suggested Elodea asked *Nimuë* to *join* the church choir? Must tell Flipper *that* bit!'. Then Finn said aloud, "And is Lance's friend Tristan also in the church choir?"

"Yes!" said Elodea, "He's *very* enthusiastic about singing! It has to be admitted that he is a little tone deaf but it doesn't really matter if you are a *bass*. Their line is mostly on one note anyway! So *good* that we have young men who keep up the old traditions in this village!"

Finn felt the full weight of being guilty of not keeping up with the old traditions while being in the village.

"Oh well, *maybe* if I'm here for a *while* I could sing *tone deaf bass* occasionally too!" he said to mollify her, "Thank you enormously for the chat and the breakfast!"

"9am practice every Sunday morning!" said Elodea, a little triumphantly, "More toast? More coffee?" she continued, waving the percolator in one hand and the toast rack in the other.

"I *really* couldn't fit anything else in!" said Finn, "I must love you and leave you before anyone else wakes up. Don't want to have Flic telling John I'm here! 9am on Sunday you say? Super!"

His heart sank at having to do Choir Practice and Church this Sunday. He supposed he could call it an Observation session. But he trotted back to the Studio cheerfully enough, feeling full and comfortable, settled into bed and found that a stomach full of caffeine did not at all disturb his deep and peaceful sleep for the next four hours. At 10am he woke up, leapt up, dressed in haste and dashed out to get the Wyching Well ready for opening. As he had expected there was no sign of Stinker but the usual strains of weird music were floating down the stairs.

Finn put his earplugs in again and started wiping down the bar, switching on the lines and cleaning the bar and loo floors.

There had been no sign of either Stinker or Nimuë downstairs by mid afternoon but the noise droned onwards upstairs.

"This is ridiculous!" FInn said to himself, "How am I meant to make progress with this case like this?"

At that point Lance popped in and seemed conversational.

"Did you *row* at Cambridge?" Finn asked, thinking that Lance had the right physique.

"No, no, takes too much time up!" said Lance, "I got a blue for ballroom dancing though!"

Finn was finding this a little boggling when Lance continued.

"My partner was a *very lovely* female PhD student who loved ballroom dancing and needed a partner. I *like* older women!" Lance confided to Finn.

Finn had to stop himself sighing at the thought of a PhD student at Cambridge being old enough to be an 'older woman'.

Lance was in a mood for confidences, he went on "I'm in love with a *much older* woman now. She's in her *late thirties*!"

"*Ah*" replied Finn, thinking that was sufficient as a reply.

"She's going to come to my twenty third birthday party on Friday evening! I'm going to have it here! Stinker will be pleased with that. He gets lots of income from birthday parties!" said Lance.

"Is there *room* for a birthday party in here?" asked Finn.

"Sure! It won't be a formal one, just anyone who is here or who turns up! A lot of people will get drinks and then spill out into the street, lots of room out there and no traffic at that time of night" replied Lance, "I'm looking forward to showing my *beautiful girlfriend* off to everyone! We are keeping it all a *secret* till then!"

"Ah!" said Finn, again, wondering if any languages did not have words like Ah, Oh and Um in them and if so how did people who spoke those languages cope, "Met her *online*?"

"Yes" said Lance, "But then, and this is an amazing coincidence, I met her for *real* on an *aeroplane* just when I was coming back from my gap year! Who could have predicted that? Now she has moved into the village to be closer to me! We are going out properly full time now!"

Finn had just been taking a swig of lemonade when Lance made this revealing speech and Finn's resulting choking fit was spectacular.

While spluttering Finn thought that Lance telling Elodea that Nimuë had a beautiful voice now made perfect sense.

"*Shhh!* Don't tell anyone else! I'm keeping it all *secret* till my birthday party!" said Lance, "I expect you get a lot of secrets confided being a barman don't you? Alcohol making people talk without realising and all that!"

"Yes, yes" answered Finn, "Lots! Lots and lots! I can assure you I'm a safe house *for all* secrets!" Finn was thinking to himself, 'Wait till Flipper hears *this* one! How is Nimuë managing to meet Lance while composing non-stop with Stinker and suspected to be meeting Mordred too? Maybe she really *is* magical and can control time? Or maybe Stinker falls asleep for a couple of hours more often than he imagines, you get people who think they never sleep when they do if they are observed or video-ed or whatever? But how come Lance hasn't heard that Nimuë is *supposed* to be *Stinker's fiancée*? Maybe she just told Lance that's wasn't true and he fell for it? She is certainly a good liar!'

Sure enough when Flipper popped into the Studio that night he was suitably impressed by the new turn of romantic events reported to him by Finn.

"How is she managing three men at once?" he asked.

"No idea, maybe she is an enchantress for real? I would swear she and Stinker have been composing nearly *all* the time. I guess he must take a nap occasionally! Perhaps sometimes the noises above are just him playing the pieces he has already written down on his cello while she claims to be popping out for some fresh air or something? Also we don't know for sure that she ever *meets* Mordred. I suppose she can send DMs and texts while Stinker is writing the music out long hand or playing the cello, he'd never notice what she was doing. This must be why Lance's trailer hydraulics seemed to have gone wrong outside the Wyching Well. Lance must have been picking her up. She probably jumped out of the window and he caught her. Then when he came back the tractor had a high fork lift attachment on it so he could get Nimuë back in through the window! Maybe they don't meet in real life much though, maybe most of it is virtual romance?"

"Video linking!" said Flipper with an appropriate leer.

"You are *so crude*!" protested Finn, "But now we have an extra dimension on this case and I am not sure if it makes it trickier or easier!"

"Let's both think on it and reconsider the matter tomorrow" said Flipper.

"You know *Tony* is back *out*?" Finn asked Flipper.

"*Good, good*!" said Flipper, "Buffy *will* be pleased!"

"So will Elodea, John, Flic and Samira!" Finn pointed out, "No case to answer apparently, charges dropped!"

"Quite right too! *I speak for the trees for the trees have no tongues!*[23]" replied Flipper.

"OK, I *have* to know" said Finn, "what is a Lorax?"

"You've never read *The Lorax*?" asked Flipper, "A story by Dr Seuss written in 1971 about the loss of ecology to industrial greed written in 1971? Now an excellent metaphor for our behaviour in continuing with Planet Destroying Emissions even if Dr Seuss is no longer perceived as entirely ideologically sound in our current times."

"No! Never heard of it!" said Finn.

"*Are you in for a treat*! I'll get you a copy!" said Flipper.

"Don't put yourself out too much!" replied Finn, "I've had enough explanation now. However lovely a story it might be it does not explain why the case was dropped."

"I think I *might* have heard that there was *no evidence*" said Flipper.

"*No evidence*?" asked Finn, "Why was he *charged* in the first place?"

"There may have been some kind of evidence once but then whatever it was, it, er, *vanished*. *****y Hackers I expect!" replied Flipper.

"*Hackers*? What about the hard copy file of evidence?" asked Finn.

"I believe it was *severely mislaid*, so severely it seems to have *totally disappeared*" replied Flipper.

"Severely mislaid files and some hackers got at the online evidence as well? Call me cynical but was it Flic's parents intervening?" asked Finn.

"Well, there's a few possible candidates who might have intervened, let me see, Flic's parents are some of the richest and most influential people in the USA, Flic's sister is in USA intelligence and his brother Paris is not without some clout at high security levels here" replied Flipper.

"So why was Tony remanded in custody *at all* then?" asked Finn.

"I suppose the security people concerned didn't know he *had* connections!" said Flipper, with a beautiful and innocent looking smile.

---

[23] The Lorax by Dr Seuss

Finn raised an eyebrow at Flipper.

Flipper sighed, "OK, then we have to consider the mysterious drag queen Morgan le Fake. I have heard tell that lots of surprisingly powerful men enjoy going to Drag Queen Clubs and similar types of meeting place."

"But I *told* Elodea we couldn't *do anything*. I told her it was *outside our remit*! You make me look dishonest!" groaned Finn.

"We *didn't* do anything" said Flipper, "*Obviously not* because we couldn't! It was just a case of nullem crimen nulla poena since praevia lege poenali[24]"

"Am I the only person on the whole Planet who still *follows rules*?" demanded Finn.

"You *don't* follow rules" retorted Flipper.

"I do!" replied Finn, throwing a pillow at him "And due to this faithful adherence to rules I am still alive whereas you are…"

He stopped because the returning pillow had just hit him full force on his face.

"And as to *why* all the evidence disappeared" said Flipper, "That must remain a mystery for all time. I find it totally *baffling* myself! *retine vim istam, falsa enim dicam, si coges*[25]"

"Hmmmph!" said Finn.

"You are a hard-hearted person! Is trying to Save the Planet a *crime*?" asked Flipper.

"Is *following rules* a crime?" asked Finn.

"Is *breaking* them one because if you persist in that one I am going to start reciting a long list of all the times I *know* about you breaking rules and then all the times when I can't prove it but I am pretty certain. It will be a long night by the time I finally finish! When did you start following the creed of *fiat justitia ruat caelum*[26]" answered Flipper.

---

[24] No crime, no punishment
[25] "Restrain yourself for if you compel me I will tell lies" Said by the Delphic Oracle and recorded by Eusebius of Caesarea

"Oh, *just leave it*! Maybe I have broken a few rules, but mostly when I did it was to rescue *you*! I'm glad Tony is home although he seems to be trying to get re-arrested by going straight back up that tree!" said Finn.

"It's OK, some people in security and law and order don't agree with killing trees and destroying the Planet either, like Elisha and his servant, Tony has an army of invisible angels watching over him now![27]" said Flipper.

"Drag Queens have more influence than I thought!" said Finn.

"Not all of them, only the *best looking* Drag Queens!" purred Flipper.

"You *are* enjoying this temporary career!" accused Finn.

"Well, dearie" replied Flipper in Morgan le Fake's voice, "I am enjoying going *clubbing* again, not often I get handed a persona who likes *clubbing* as much as *she* does. You should see me whooping it up on the dance floor! Tremendous fun! But wait for *this*, guess the name of the closed entry Drag Queen Club I have been going to!"

"No idea! Men in Dresses?" suggested Finn.

"No, no, this is going to absolutely *creep* you out, you *superstitious* old thing, you, it's the *Belvedere*!" said Flipper.

"*Belvedere*, as in *Sir Belvedere*, as in Arthurian legends?" demanded Finn.

"Yes, but it's *not* actually an Arthurian reference, it happens to be named after the owner, he's *called* Belvedere!" answered Flipper.

"Belvedere being a *person* is even worse! Belvedere isn't a *knight* is he?" asked Finn.

"Could be! He is pretty high up in the business world in his other life. Could well have been knighted! His *drag* name is going to creep you out *even more*, it's Lady Elaine of Shall I. 'Shall I' instead of 'Shalott', see!" said Flipper.

---

[26] "Let justice be done should the sky fall" attributed to Caesoninus
[27] 2 Kings 6 v 17

"Yes, I managed to grasp that bit, thank you!" replied Finn, "*You* don't find even more Arthurian references popping up at all unlikely?"

"Oh no, I can see the point of this one being used entirely. Medieval Drag! The Headgear! The Dresses! *Sublime!*" replied Flipper.

Finn brought the pillow back into play and banged Flipper on the head, "You are remembering this is just role play, aren't you?" he pleaded sounding rather anxious.

"I *am*! I *promise!*" said Flipper sounding very serious, but he gave a very Morgan le Fake giggle at the end and ruined the entire statement.

"I told you that purple flowered running suit was a mistake! One step leads to another! How are you managing being in the Wyching Well in the afternoon, coming here *and* clubbing?" demanded Finn.

"There is nothing wrong with embracing my destiny!" said Flipper, "Perhaps this *is* who I am! The Belvedere is open *all* hours of the night, it only really gets going after about four a.m., so I can fit it in with looking after you and all my other activities" replied Flipper, "And I'm *not* managing, I'm *permanently tired*! Oh, look at the time! Must get going!"

Flipper bounced across the room with no sign of his claimed exhaustion and let himself out to cycle back to Oxford, get changed and go clubbing.

Finn was not going to bed either. He rushed around putting on dark clothes so he could go and have a little secret mooch around the back garden of the White House.

"Must remember to not fall over the foundations on this moonless dark and cloudy night! That was very good advice from Flipper. What perfect conditions for a bit of sleuthing though!" Finn said to himself.

Shortly afterwards Finn was sitting in The White House garden, at the base of the high back garden wall, completely concealed by the darkness. He could smell the wet garden and the scent of geraniums flowering beside the wall. From the pond in the garden came the sound of frogs croaking loudly.

Time passed. A wandering beetle found Finn's leg of major interest. "Just don't bring your friends the ants round next" he hissed at it.

Then, at last, just as Finn was about to nod off to sleep and had decided he must give up, Finn heard the sound of two pairs of feet creeping along softly on the other side of the garden wall and continuing past him. A few yards further along from him two more dark figures threw themselves over the wall, one turning back to help the second one down by catching her in his arms.

"But this is *the White House garden*" said Nimuë's voice.

"That's right!" said Lance's voice.

"Where is this secret place you all used to meet up in and canoodle when you were teenagers then? Not inside the *house* surely?" demanded Nimuë.

"No, of course not *inside* the house! What do you take us for? And we didn't necessarily *canoodle*, we were only kids. Just *fun*, you know, messing about!" protested Lance.

"So where is this place then?" Nimuë asked again.

Lance led her forwards by the hand, carefully skirting the old foundations, "Here!" he announced, bending forward and pulling at a huge old iron ring hidden under the grass.

"No! No!" she squeaked.

"No what?" asked Lance, dropping the ring again before the trapdoor had lifted and turning round towards her.

"Not *underground*? Surely not *underground*?" squeaked Nimuë.

"Yes, underground, but it's a good solid building, it's the old cellars from the house that was here before! All clean and dry, no one ever uses them now!" replied Lance.

"Not *cellars*! No *cellars*!" whimpered Nimuë, "I don't like spiders and there might be ghosts!"

"There aren't any ghosts in the cellars, the ghosts appear in the house itself. They are the people who used to live in the old house here, years ago, in Victorian times, the Oldies in the Village say it's because they got burned alive and cannot find peace so they are still walking the Earth!" said Lance, "But you weren't worried about *the ghosts* in the house! *Remember*! You said your parents have rented this house for you to live in while you are studying for a Masters in Astrophysics because they don't think Music is a proper subject and you didn't believe in ghosts so it could have as many as it liked! That's why you haven't told your parents you are composing a brilliant new work with Stinker's help and you have to live in the Wyching Well to do that! *They* think you live here and are working towards your Masters! That's why I had to come and see if there was any post here the other day!"

Lance stopped because he had run out of breath.

"Yes, yes, that's all *true*! But no cellars, no, no" whimpered Nimuë, "I'm scared, Lance, I'm scared, take me away! Let's go to the woods, or your haybarn or somewhere! We have to hurry because that drugged cocoa I gave to Stinker will not last very long!"

"If you *must*, come on then, I'll hoist you back over that wall!" said Lance, "Let's go find a barn, Tristan's is the closest, that will *do!*"

But he sounded disappointed that his romantic revisiting of the past had been so thoroughly rejected.

Lance lifted Nimuë up so she could sit on the top of the wall and then climbed over himself while she sat there so he could catch her as she landed. Finn heard them creeping away behind the back wall. There was a sweet smell of crushed wet grass where their feet passed.

'How very *edifying* that conversation was!' he said to himself, 'What a pathological liar Nimuë is!'

Finn was just wondering whether to go and explore the cellar entrance himself when he heard another pair of feet approaching along the back of the wall. This pair continued did not climb over the wall but unlocked the back gate.

Even in the thick darkness Finn could see a white mop of hair on top of a very short man's head. The man was walking as if he belonged there, briskly, with a young man's stride, not with the usual tottering steps of Phineas Floyd, he did not look old or even so sick that he still needed to shield from Covid. Nonetheless Finn could see that the man matched the description of Phineas Floyd that the inhabitants of Little Wychwell had supplied. Finn sniffed the air, yes, that was the very strong smell of the Designer aftershave that Elodea had mentioned Phineas always wore when he answered the door to take groceries in. Would any other inhabitant of Little Wychwell would have worn aftershave that expensive when trotting round fields behind gardens in the middle of a dark night? Frederick Heron might but he was entirely the wrong shape, this man was small and wiry.

'I think we can call that positive id' Finn said to himself, 'The size, the hair, or presumably the *wig*, the particular aftershave! It's Phineas Floyd and I am pretty positive that his real name is Mordred!"

The man crossed to where Lance and Nimuë had stood, fished in the grass and pulled on the huge brass ring. Then he swung back an obviously very heavy cover, laid it on the grass, disappeared slowly down a set of steps and then, with some difficulty as it was so unwieldly, he pulled the trapdoor back over the gap above his head and closed the entrance again.

But Finn had already heard the sound of many small oil fuelled electricity generators all running at once.

'What a satisfactory explanation!' he said to himself, 'The oil is powering dozens, maybe hundreds of little generators and it must be powering something else. A huge bank of servers I would guess, they swallow a lot of power. My sound recorder will have picked up the noise, my night camera will have got the people, it just all needs analysing! We will have to get a specialist team in to disable whatever racket he is running from here. I expect it's what Flip and I suspected, another crypto exchange for laundering dodgy money or fleecing innocent people into handing their savings over! I expect our Mordred is making millions!'

Finn sat there a while longer hoping that Phineas/Mordred might reappear.

Instead Nimuë appeared, alone, using the gate to get into the garden this time.

She too crossed the lawn, heaved the trapdoor up, impressing Finn again with her evident muscle power, and also disappeared down into the cellars.

'What next? This is going splendidly tonight! Maybe Mordred and Nimuë would like to both come back up and make a full confession right away to save time?' Finn said to himself, 'Got to admire the girl's stamina, she *is* playing all three of them! She must be part of the crypto exchange fraud too. The woman must be made of iron! Most people would be exhausted just living with Stinker, let alone keeping Lance on a string and still being Mordred's girlfriend *and* being a master crypto criminal *and* taking illegal drugs *and* singing for days on end like that, any one of which would seem wearing enough!'

Finn decided he had done enough for one night, the sky was starting to lighten towards dawn, he must go. He could hardly storm the cellars himself without back up and that side of the investigation needed the right specialists, it was fortunate that Mordred and Nimue seemed so sure no one would guess what was happening in the cellars that they appeared to have no security. This sort of high tech skills required to get enough evidence and shut the operation down were right out of Finn's remit and if he himself tried to gather any more information now he would risk Mordred panicking and wiping the servers before the evidence had been taken. 'Not a big gang operation' Finn said to himself, 'only trying to deal with a few of the intelligentsia, it will not need full back up forces'.

Finn remembered that he would be rather occupied that evening himself, "I've got Lance's party to deal with, that will be pretty wild I expect, too many drinks, too many drunk people! I wonder what Nimuë used to drug Stinker with? It must be something quite instant, that will be why Stinker thinks he has not been to sleep, or not more than a very short nap. I hope Stinker's going to be in a fit state to help draw pints by this evening! He can jolly well turn up and help tonight if I have to go upstairs and drag him down myself!'

He looked at his watch, "Just about time!" he said, "I suppose the good folk of Little Wychwell will believe I am taking a long cycle ride for exercise at this time of morning if I am seen. I have to go and find Flipper so he can get Mike and Ed in. Plenty of time to do that and get back by 11am, unless of course Flipper is still whooping it up on the dancefloor in his closed entry nightclub!"

Finn flung himself quietly over the back wall of the White House and went to find his bicycle.

As FInn cycled along he felt satisfied that the case would soon be closed and also confident that all problems would be solved in one go. Whatever IT scam they were running in the cellars would be closed down. Mordred and Nimue would discover this had happened and take the hint without putting up a fight. They were too artistic and intelligent to attempt any form of attack on security forces. Instead they would both head straight to an airport and vanish off abroad again in a Mordred Private Jet. There would be no confrontation, no arrests, no prosecutions required, no fuss, no danger. Finn began to wonder what his next case would be. It was a fine morning, he was enjoying the exercise, he was happy.

Chapter Eight

Lance turned up at the Wyching Well at about three p.m. to start preparing for his birthday party. He had a huge trailer on the back of his equally huge tractor.

"I've got ten barrels of best bitter in the back" Lance said to Finn, "But I'll leave them all in there for now, no room in here for that many, we are going to drink Stinker's stock *dry* tonight and then some! These are a gift from me for Stinker for letting me have the party here, he can charge the usual price for the pints from them!"

Before Finn could reply with appropriate thanks Lance's Mother bustled in with a huge white cardboard box.

"Here's the *cake*, love!" Mrs Boswell said to her son, "Not a birthday party without cake, now, is it?" she said to Finn, "Lance says he's *too old* but you *can't* be too old for cake!"

"Thank you very much, Mrs Boswell, that's *very* kind of you!" Finn replied, "Will you and Mr Boswell be along later this evening for the party?"

"No, thank *you*!" she replied, "We will be having his *family* birthday party on Sunday, I'm afraid the Wyching Well is a little *wild* for *us*!"

Finn looked around at Old Alf, Robin, Jake and a few of their other elderly friends, chatting in a leisurely way over their pints. Finn thought that if only the Wyching Well was a little *wilder* he might not nearly nod off quite so often. A collection of suitable sarcastic ripostes flew through his mind and then he remembered that Stinker *must* keep in with the Village Elders, however rude they were about his delightful and well ordered establishment, so Finn merely smiled and nodded at Lance's Mother.

Mrs Boswell gave Lance a very loud and very demonstrative kiss on the cheek and hurried out before the tainting atmosphere of the Wyching Well might damage her.

"*Mothers*!" groaned Lance, blushing, "She *knows* I hate cake! She continually tries to reduce me to about three years old!"

"I'm sure some of the people at the party like cake" soothed Finn, "And your Mother is quite *right*" he added, thinking he should support Mothers as they were wonderful and essential people and *especially* in case what he was saying got repeated to Mrs Boswell, "*It isn't a birthday party without a cake.*"

Finn continued in a coaxing and encouraging tone, "Look it's a *wonderful* cake! It's got a model of *you* on a *tractor* on it and twenty-three candles and she's even included some serviettes to put the slices on when we cut it!"

Lance groaned even more loudly, "Me on a tractor! That's not me! It looks like someone from Postman Pat[28]" He put his head down on the bar and looked a picture of misery.

"I'll have a knife ready, we can have it mid evening!" announced Finn, in a bracing tone of voice, "Please remember to thank her from me! You *will* enjoy blowing the candles out, *you'll see*! Don't look a gift horse in the mouth. By the time you get to *my* age you will *appreciate* someone *bothering* to make you a birthday cake!"

Lance remained despairing. Finn felt old.

"Cheer up lad!" Old Alf called across to Lance, "Mardy toddlers your age usually like birthday cakes! Just be grateful your Mum cares that much about you!"

Everyone else in the bar laughed. Lance looked as if his cup of humiliation was now brimming over.

"OK Lance, I think we had better get the barrels into the back garden" said Finn, hoping to distract Lance from his embarrassment, "Otherwise it will take too long to get them all off the trailer when we need them and we might find someone else has collected them for free in the mean time. We can manage to roll them round the back between us, I think!"

---

[28] A stop motion animated children's TV program first written by John Cunliffe and animated by Ivor Wood and produced by Woodland Animations and later produced by Cosgrove Hall Films. Still being shown on CBeebies.

"Anyone likely to nick them off the trailer will be *inside* the party so I will be having words with the likely suspects if the barrels have gone. It would be easier to roll them in from the back garden this evening instead of lifting them down from the trailer though. Right, let's go!" said Lance, recovering at the thought of a useful physical activity that acknowledged his age and strength and also about the amount of beer he would be able to enjoy later.

By the time Lance and Finn had lifted all ten barrels off the trailer and rolled and lifted them to stand near the back door they were both out of breath.

As they closed up the back of the trailer Lance begged Finn "Can't you just accidentally sit on that cake? Or fall over it? Or forget to get it out? Or something?"

"No!" said Finn, "Your Mother is *bound* to ask people whether they *liked* the cake. I will serve it at an *appropriate* time"

But as things turned out that evening Finn's prediction was wrong and Lance's wishes to not have ceremonial candle blowing and cake cutting were about to be fulfilled.

"You know what?" said Lance.

"No" said Finn.

"It would be much better to line all these barrels up along the wall inside the bar instead of having them outside the back door. Then people can use them as seats and it will be much faster to shift them over to the lines from there!" said Lance.

"Brilliant thinking!" said Finn.

They moved all the barrels again.

Finn was now hoping that Lance would not think of any other even better places, upstairs for example, but the barrel position seemed to be finally satisfactory.

By eight p.m. the Wyching Well was crammed with enthusiastic drinkers. Morgan le Fake had materialised and was jammed at a table sharing just two chairs with Alf, Robin and Jake. Stinker had still not appeared.

Finn was now annoyed, 'Where is Stinker? He knows it's Lance's party! Also Flipper could come and help me serve if he got off his lazy backside and round the back of the bar! I'm sure Morgan le Fake can manage to pull pints. Look at Flipper, lolling about enjoying himself!' The orders were piling up, the customers were getting restless. Fortunately Tristan noticed the chaos and without being asked came round to the back of the bar to help Finn.

"Where is Nimuë?" asked Lance, materialising in front of Finn, "She promised, she promised to come to the party tonight and formally announce our relationship!"

"I think she must be upstairs, probably just titivating her clothes and make up, you know what women are like" soothed Finn, while pulling two pints at once and really not caring where Nimuë might be unless she was likely to come and help serve behind the bar.

"Nimuë is having a relationship with Lance and the whole of the rest of the army!" said Tristan to Finn sarcastically.

Luckily Lance was already at the door at the bottom of the stairs and wrenching it open and so did not hear Tristan.

"Nimuë!" Lance called upstairs, "Nimuë! Are you coming to this party or not?"

Finn heard her voice float downstairs to him "Oh Lance, is it tonight? I forgot all about it! I cannot join you just yet, I am clutched in the arms of genius!"

"You'll be clutched by my arms in a way you don't enjoy at all if you don't turn up soon" Lance muttered to himself as he closed the door to the stairs and turned away. His face darkened with rage.

Finn decided this might be a good moment to get the Birthday Cake out as a diversion from Nimuë's intrigues. But Finn was just about to lift the box onto the bar top when two of the church bells started to ring, a high note followed by a low note, repeated again and again.

It was the notes of an emergency siren rather than the slow and solemn tolling that still announced a death in Little Wychwell. Finn wondered if perhaps it was bell ringing practice night and this was a new exercise for the Bell Ringers? But when he looked round most of the bell ringers were in the bar.

"*That's it boys!*" announced Old Alf, standing up and banging the table for attention, Alf climbed up on a chair in a wobbly way and then gained stability, he raised his voice above the hubbub, "That's the Vicar and the Warden ringing the bells for us! It's *Pile On time!* Come on Lance boy, you can take us all in your big trailer! *Everybody Out!*"

The entire crowd became excited and started to yell "The Bells! The Bells! Pile On! Pile On!" as if it was a Football chant.

Lance was completely distracted from any bad temper, he looked as alive and excited and thrilled as the rest of them. Lance fished his tractor keys out of his pocket and made it to the door first.

All the villagers slammed their pints down on the nearest surface and headed out, jamming themselves in the front door, as though the Wyching Well was on fire.

Old Alf, who seemed to have taken charge, as the oldest Little Wychweller in the building, yelled, "One at a time! One at a time! You are just wasting time all rushing and crowding like that! Order! Order!"

Then Alf turned to Finn, "*You stay here, boy!*" he said, "And if anyone else from the Village happens to come in and hasn't heard the bells then you tell them it's *Pile On Time*. They'll know what to do!"

Alf grabbed Morgan le Fake by the arm and took her with him.

"I'll take the Daisymobile!" simpered Morgan, "You don't want to be rattling round in the back of a trailer at your age, Alf, and I don't want to risk my clothes getting all covered with whatever Lance had in it last!"

"I *suppose* so!" said Alf, a little grumpily, "But it would be much more fun in with the rest of the crowd!"

"You can give me *all* the *directions* you like on the way!" breathed Morgan le Fake.

"I'll look forward to *that* bit!" said Alf.

Morgan le Fake blew a kiss back to Finn as they slowly progressed through the door behind the rest at Alf's top speed.

Finn had never seen the Wyching Well clear so quickly "I wish they would do this at Closing Time" he said to himself.

FInn heard Lance's tractor rev up and roar away with the excited cheers of the trailer passengers ringing out over the engine noise. Finn wondered if he was the only person in the World who had no idea what was going on. Clearly an emergency of some sort! But the Wyching Well itself could not be in danger, Alf would never have left him inside it if it was, he was sure of that.

"A Pylon?" he wondered to himself, "What *sort* of Pylon? An electricity Pylon? Or is it the local name for some animal I have never heard about? *Where* have they all gone? Why has Buffy never told me about this strange custom? Is it a birthday party tradition? Does this always happen at birthday parties? Perhaps that's it! Perhaps it's like the Bumps?"

But there was no-one there from the village to ask.

A few minutes later Stinker staggered down the stairs.

"Just come to help with the party" Stinker announced to Finn, then he looked round and realised the whole place was empty, "Where *is* everyone? Did no-one turn up? How terrible! Lance will be upset!"

"No, it's a Pylon!" said Finn.

"A python? A *python* has escaped? I didn't even know anyone kept them? Did it escape from the Vicar's animal hospital? Was he nursing it back to health?" replied Stinker.

"Not a python! A *pylon*!" replied Finn, "Didn't you hear the bells? Do you *know* what a Little Wychwell Pylon is?"

"No" said Stinker.

"You're a lot of help! *Neither* of us know what everyone else is doing! Where is *Nimuë*?" asked Finn.

"Gone out!" said Stinker, "*Just* after Lance called up the stairs. She couldn't hear herself singing over the noise down here so she was really furious and went out, she said there was no point in continuing to attempt composition."

'Let us be thankful for small mercies' said Finn to himself.

"How did she get out without coming through here?" Finn asked Stinker.

"She nips in and out by the upstairs window" Stinker replied, "She's so thin and supple she can do it quite easily. We would probably both get stuck in the frame. She has a piece of rope tied to the bed so she can let herself down on it and then she shins back up the wall using the same rope when she returns. Then she puts it back under the bed. Very nimble person! It saves her disturbing me from the noise of all the doors opening and shutting when I am writing her compositions down. She usually only uses it for night time wanders so she can gain inspiration from Nature!"

'Has she gone to the Pylon with Lance?' wondered Finn to himself, 'Did she relent of her hard-hearted behaviour to him after all?'

Stinker surveyed the mess of half empty glasses and chairs that had been knocked over in the hurry to leave, "I'm going to make myself a coffee and go and sit outside and drink it in peace. I expect they will all be back in a few minutes. Probably some kind of tradition even if it isn't one I have heard about yet. I've been here for years and never known *this* happen before. Rushing out and leaving their glasses part full is very odd! Who can guess what they might do in this place from time to time, I expect Buffy knows what it is, but then he is probably *at* it!"

Stinker made a coffee and went and sat in peace on the wall outside the Wyching Well in the cool evening air. He had missed this activity lately. He liked sitting alone sometimes. He was hardly ever alone anymore and when he *was* on his own he was so tired he seemed to fall straight asleep or else he had to write out pages and pages of manuscript in a fair hand.

"I *love* Nimuë" Stinker told himself aloud, "but she has taken over *my whole life*. I miss being *me*. I miss it *very* much. I suppose this is how it is when you find your partner for life. They *take* your life but you get to be *loved*? It is good to be loved! But…"

Stinker closed his eyes and enjoyed the solitude.

Meanwhile back in the bar Finn had switched the television on for amusement while he lethargically started to gather up the scattered glasses, throw the remaining contents away and put them through the glass washer. He did not get the impression that any of the missing drinkers would return that evening. He might as well clear the place up now instead of later. It was a shame about the lost takings from drinks sales that evening but at least Stinker still had ten free barrels of beer against the wall. The local news came on the TV.

"In breaking news" said the clipped voice of the announcer "the Littie Wychwell and Upper Storkmorton villagers have turned out in huge numbers to defend their Boundary Oak. The usually rival villagers have all turned out together to defend the historic Boundary Marker between their parishes from a felling team hired by Property Developers who have bought the field in which it stands and planned to secretly fell it this evening. There have been small numbers of Ecological Protestors sitting up the tree for weeks but the Developers had brought in teams of security staff to remove them. The tree is now completely full of Little Wychwell villagers on one side and Upper Storkmorton villagers on the other and the felling teams have been unable to proceed! Among the Little Wychwell contingent is the very glamorous Drag Queen Morgan le Fake."

To Finn's horror there was Flipper, legs over a branch, frilly knickers and suspenders showing beneath his skirt, waving and blowing kisses to the camera.

When he peered at the screen at close range he could see everyone from Lance's party and then many more villagers. The branches were completely packed and around the base of the tree there was a huge crowd of people who could not even fit in the tree. Surely that was Buffy sitting next to Tony on a higher branch?

"The felling crew say it is essential to cut down the tree so that vital infrastructure can be constructed to facilitate building much needed houses" the voice continued, "They say that security reinforcements are on their way and the small crowd will be dispersed."

"Not 'much needed houses', ' not at all needed luxuries that no one local can afford to buy'!" shouted someone from the branches of the tree.

There was a huge cheer in support of the statement.

"You can't arrest *all* of us!" yelled another voice.

There was an even bigger cheer.

"We are speaking for the oak for the oak has no tongue[29]!" yelled a young voice from a very high branch.

Even more tumultuous cheers and applause.

Then the entire crowd started to chant "What do we need? We need trees! What do we need? We need trees!"

'Good luck trying to *disperse* that lot!' thought Finn.

The news report ended.

Finn giggled to himself as he now knew what a Pylon meant In Little Wychwell, he had been suffering from a phonetics error, it was not a Pylon but a Pile On.

'I am *losing* my brain!' he told himself, "I have been in this village far too long *again*!"

****

Half an hour later, surrounded by a deafening noise of chants and protest singing, Lance was perched on a branch next to Tristan in the tree. Tristan was chanting and singing enthusiastically but Lance was still sad.

---

[29] "I speak for the trees for the trees have no tongues" The Lorax by Dr Seuss.

"Why *didn't* she come to my party?" he grieved.

"Because, *thickhead*, she has got *at least* two more boyfriends as well as you!" Tristan replied, who, having managed to drink eight pints already that evening, thought it was time to face his friend with harsh reality.

"No, no, you are *wrong*! Stinker *isn't* her boyfriend, they are *just* composing together, and there *isn't another* one!" said Lance, sounding confused.

"That's what *you* think! I wasn't going to say anything since you were so happy with *one third* of her and it seemed like *harmless fun* but if you are going to get all distressed and moody it's time you knew the *truth*" said his heartless friend, "Not only does Stinker say she has said she is going to *marry* him but she has also been spotted nipping in and out the back of *Phineas Floyd's* house and for *all I know* there are *others* as well!" replied his heartless friend.

"*Phineas Floyd*? He's *miles* too old for her and he's *not well enough* to have affairs!" protested Lance.

"That's what *you* think. Don't forget *she's* miles too old for *you* too and some women like frail old men with money, they think the money might all be about to drop into their laps! I have heard that old Phineas isn't ill at all, just a hypochondriac, but that he is *very* rich! *Forget her*! Get someone decent not someone *using* you as a *toyboy*! You can have your pick of *lovely* Little Wychwell girls, Louise, Emily, Fran...." said Tristan.

"I'll go and see her *right now*! I'll have it out with her! I'm off to the Wyching Well *right now*! She'll be sorry if she is playing fast and loose with *me*!" interrupted Lance, "*I'll be back*!"

"Don't, Lance*, don't*! She isn't *worth it*!" said Tristan, wondering what terrible consequences his words might cause, but it was too late, Lance had already jumped to the ground.

Tristan sighed and then he comforted himself with "Lance had to find out some time, might as well be today as later! He won't do her any harm! He's too kind hearted and Stinker is much bigger and stronger than he looks and he must be there too. He will stop Lance doing anything violent."

Lance struggled through the crowd and out to his waiting tractor. He unhitched the trailer.

The security guards and tree felling crew cheered as Lance got into the cab, turned the engine on and started to leave, "One down, soon clear the rest" one of them yelled.

Lance stopped the tractor right next door to them, unwound the cab window and said, "Don't think you've seen the back of me. I've just got to go and check on one of our in-calf heifers and make sure she's not calving yet, I'll be back, don't you worry yourselves!"

Lance put his foot down hard on the accelerator and scattered the Security Guards and the felling crew as he drove furiously out on to the road and back to Little Wychwell. Lance laughed at the sight of their frightened faces. But it was an angry laugh with no humour in it.

Tristan's fears about what Lance might do in his current temper grew by the minute after his friend left. Tristan's loyalty to Lance required him to keep a dutiful silence but after half an hour of worry Tristan decided he had better make sure nothing terrible had happened in Little Wychwell. So Tristan readjusted his position, much to the annoyance of those he climbed over as they balanced on a branch, and managed to get next to Morgan le Fake.

"Sorry, sorry!" Tristan finished apologising to those he had just stood on. He turned to Morgan le Fake and lowered his voice to say "I'm a bit worried about what Lance is *doing* right now!" "I *may* have said something to him that *upset* him! I can't leave the tree myself because I am a Villager and must *not* abandon the rest in a Pile On, even if Lance did, and nor can *any* of the others, but you can because you are not a villager. Can you make an excuse and go and find out what Lance is up to? I'll explain…." Tristan said to Morgan and then continued to fill Morgan in with the details.

**

We must now return to the Wyching Well as it was at the end of the TV news broadcast.

Finn had very little time to wonder about the TV news and its possible consequences because Stinker burst in through the front door looking wild and frantic.

Stinker turned quickly and locked and bolted the front door and then rushed across and locked and bolted the back door.

"*Quickly!*" Stinker cried to Finn, "Help me stack these full barrels *in front of the window*, two barrels high so they cover most of the window over!"

Finn did not like to ask *why* he should do this, Stinker's behaviour was so unusual that he felt he had better comply even if Stinker had gone completely mad. They moved and lifted the barrels.

"Now!" said Stinker, breathing rather hard, "Come on! Upstairs! Quick! Quick! Get Nimuë's rope pulled back up! Get the table and the bed against that window! Make sure no one can get in that way!"

Finn and Stinker rushed up to do this, then rushed down again and finally both sat on the bottom of the stairs.

"This is about the safest place in the building" Stinker said to Finn, "We can get upstairs from and if we have to maybe we can break out by making a hole out on to the roof, it's not a strong ceiling! Otherwise as a last resort we might be thin enough to be able to climb the chimney to get out from the fireplace here! It's a good old fashioned one, the sort they used to sweep by sending little boys up it!"

"Stinker, old fellow, *what are you going on about*?" soothed Finn, "what is *happening*?"

"*Nimuë! Nimuë!* She is trying to *finish me off*! I knew it! *I am Merlin*! It is the Legend *come to life*! First she has trapped me for weeks and stolen my composition skills and now she is going to kill me! It is all *true*!" said Stinker.

"Why do you think that?" asked Finn, in a calming voice, thinking he urgently needed to get hold of a mental health team.

"I dreamt last night that Nimuë was riding on a gigantic wolf! In my dream she raced towards me on it with someone else riding on it too, just behind her! The man behind her was that *toad* Mordred from Oxford! The wolf was about to grab my throat and kill me when I woke up!" replied Stinker, "I was in a cold sweat, but all was quiet in real life, there Nimuë was, just sitting by the table, perfectly gentle. I had fallen asleep with my head on the table, you understand, I do that sometimes. But everything was safe!"

"But that was just a *dream*, it wasn't *true*. There are *no* wolves big enough for two people to ride on!" said Finn, as serenely as he could, taking Stinker's hand and patting it gently. Had Nimuë been feeding him hallucinogenic drugs? Was he having a flashback?

"That's what you think! You go upstairs and look through the bit of the window we couldn't quite cover. There is a wolf big enough to ride on out there! And Nimuë is riding it with another person! The wolf is not racing along, it's only lumbering slowly! But it's *there*! It's *real*!" replied Stinker.

As if to prove his point a loud thump was heard as something heavy collided with the front door. Finn rushed upstairs as commanded and craned sideways through the gap between the bed and the chair to see what was outside.

Stinker was not mad after all. There was a *huge* wolf outside, even if it was a deformed metallic wolf, a robotic wolf, with jointed crooked legs and flashing red eyes. Nimuë and someone who had to be Mordred, no longer disguised as Phineas Floyd, were both riding on the wolf's back, one behind the other.

The wolf had now shambled back to the opposite side of the road and was about to make another attempt at the front door and try to ram it again.

The wolf lurched forwards, very unsteadily, increased its speed to a quick walk and slammed its head into the Wyching Well door for the second time. The impact with the door made its legs buckle, it stumbled, wobbled from side to side, regained a vertical position and then retreated backwards for its next attempt. Mordred and Nimuë were rocking and jolting about on its back but staying on.

"Robot makers have got a lot of work to do on the movement aspect, fortunately for Stinker and myself! What a wreck of an animal it is! It looks like a pile of wobbling junk trying to move about. Those two must be strapped in" mused Finn to himself "Or they would fall off every time it rocks let alone when it hits the door like that! Why do they build these ridiculous pretend animals? They should use their brains instead of trying to create life as it is currently known. God complex I suppose! They should produce something that can move effectively without legs, not some pseudo four-legged creature suffering from multiple physical disabilities!"

"Come out, you *cowards*!" shouted Mordred, "Don't think we don't know it was *you two*! It must have been *you two*! No one else in this damned village could have done it! This wolf is armed, if you do not come out and die like men then we will come in and kill you both inside!"

'Hmm! I guess our specialists have been in and his servers have been sabotaged effectively. So much for my idea that those two would just fade out and make a dash for the nearest airport. He and Nimuë must have come directly from his house on that thing. They cannot have gone near the cellars or they would have encountered our saboteurs in there and been arrested already. I was not expecting Mordred to go for a violent response. He must have sent Nimuë a message earlier to tell her to come and join him, that's why she dashed out! I had better get back down before Stinker does something foolishly heroic like boldly going outside singing some aria suitable for those about to get killed!' thought Finn.

Finn dashed back down.

"What is he saying? What are we *supposed* to have done?" asked Stinker, "*Did* we do something? Did I *sleepwalk* and do something terrible?"

"I don't know what we are supposed to have done and, no, *we* haven't done anything!" replied Finn, thinking that was the fastest way to deal with these awkward questions and also being very thankful that Stinker had experienced such a strange and prophetic dream and been so effective at knowing how to build suitable defences in a hurry. Or was it a true dream? Was Nimuë talking to Mordred on her mobile earlier today, not last night at all? Was Stinker asleep just before she went out? Did his unconscious mind hear what they were both saying?

"Is that man Mordred?" Finn asked.

"Yes, it's Mordred!" said Stinker, "Mordred who used to read Music with myself and Nimuë. He's older of course but it's unmistakeably him! He's the rat who went out with Nimuë before I did! But Finn! His name is *Mordred*! *Arthur* is going to *die* as well as *Merlin*! Did *you* say one of your names was *Arthur*?"

"No!" said Finn "It isn't. There is *no one* here called Arthur! You are not called Merlin either! Neither of us is going to die. Whichever way I die eventually I adamantly refuse to be killed by a deformed robot wolf!"

As he said this an automatic gun attachment on the wolf fired a shot through the glass of the window and hit one of barrels of beer. It burst through the thick metal. Best bitter under pressure fired back at the attackers in a forceful if thin stream.

"Don't think that will stop us!" screamed Mordred, remaining defiant, despite being completely soaked in sticky beer.

"Hmmm! The wolf is not just a battering ram. It's armed!" said Finn, "That makes things a little different. Keep down at floor level old chap!"

Chapter Nine

"Keep down!" said Finn to Stinker again, giving him a sharp yank on to the floor to encourage this behaviour.

Finn thought he should give Stinker praise for his earlier actions to strengthen his resolve and courage, they would have to work together if that object broke into the building and Stinker, lying prone and seeming inclined to sob, did not yet resemble the ideal partner in a fight, "Awfully well done, Stinker old fellow, by the way, absolutely brilliant organisation of rapid defences!"

"Now that's a funny thing!" replied Stinker, brightening a little, "You may be wondering *why* I had already planned what to do? Well, I have often worried about ram raids on the Wyching Well to steal the cash out of the till and the spirits and that sort of stuff, so I have had this little plan ready for some time in case anyone said there *were* ram raiders in the area so I could set all the defences up before I went to bed. But I would never have got everything in place *in time* without *you*!"

Another bullet pinged through another pane of glass, another barrel was holed and more beer flew out in response. This time the beer seemed to be hitting Nimuë, judging by her cries of anger and distress.

"I don't know *how* I am going to pay for the new windows!" wailed Stinker, who was now completely prone on the floor.

"*That*" said Finn, "Is currently the *least* of our worries! Whatever! I expect I can put it on my expenses. Remember, *neither of us are called Merlin or Arthur*!" said Finn "That's good! We should get out alive!"

"Your *expenses*?" faltered Stinker.

"You must know I'm actually at work. I bet Barnabus has blown the gaffe on that one before now, he is the most hopeless secret keeper I have ever met!" replied Finn.

"Can't you put out an emergency call for help on anything then?" asked Stinker.

"No, I am strictly and completely off grid for this investigation. The other side have got too good at tracking if modern communications methods. I could set my overnight alarm and then get it to make a phone ringing noise, afraid that's my best offer" Finn replied, "Unfortunately we had labelled this operation as very low risk to personnel! Slight miscalculation on the psychology of the opposition!"

"Who is your local back up then? You must have one!" persisted Stinker.

"Yes, but Flipper is half way up a tree in a set of petticoats pretending to be a Drag Queen!" said Finn.

"And I don't use social media because I am paranoid about people like you and hackers and things so I can't use that! The phone, the landline phone! I have a phone! We can phone, we can ring the Police!" said Stinker.

Stinker dashed behind the bar and picked the phone up.

"*Dead*!" he said.

He looked at the phone wire, "When did you last use this phone?"

"I don't know, to order some beer I suppose!" replied Finn.

"Do you think I have forgotten to pay the bill? Or has Nimuë cut it off somehow?" said Stinker.

The wolf hit the door again. It was achieving harder impacts with each new blow.

"I expect Mordred's wolf shot through the wire from outside!" said Finn, "Or pulled it down on the way here or something like that! Phone wires are quite frail and only very low current so detaching them is trivial and non-dangerous to self!"

"*Mordred*! He's behind all this! I bet he got Nimue to come and pretend to be my girlfriend again! Never liked him! He's very clever you know! Not just musical but very good at IT! Even if he didn't look quite similar still I could tell him anywhere! People age but their *voice music* is still the same tune! That little swine! He once pinched my composition in the style of Mozart and passed it off as his at a tutorial! So I didn't have one and had to make a different one up on the spot! Spoilt little brat! He and Nimuë must have got back together after Oxford? I expect she turned up just after I bought this place because she had had a spat with him and then they made it up. *Tallis*! I *knew* he wasn't her favourite composer! She *hasn't* been alone trying to return to me all these years! This is the last straw! If he breaks my beautiful ancient door, if he damages it, I'll, I'll..." said Stinker, his voice muffled a little as he had resumed a position face down on the floor.

Stinker broke off as there was a huge impact on the door. The impact saved Finn having to reply to Stinker's tirade. The hinges were now bending alarmingly. The Robowolf's speed and aim were improving, it seemed only a matter of time before it succeeded.

"It's a good job they didn't think to ram the walls instead of the door" said Stinker, "I reckon they could have gone straight through them with the first blow, they are only wattle and daub for the most part."

"*Don't give them ideas*!" said Finn.

"Why don't we just nip out through the back door and over the back fence?" asked Stinker.

"Flipper is *bound* to turn up shortly, he always turns up like a bad penny eventually, and until then we must put our faith in the skill of our ancient forebears at hinge and door construction. That wolf may be able to move much faster in pursuit than we have seen, even if it's ungainly. And it's armed." said Finn, "I would rather wait for Flipper to arrive if we *can* hold out that long. Plus for all we know Nimuë has tricked the very besotted Lance into coming back from the Boundary Oak to help her and *he* could be out the back! He is very smitten and very young. Even if he was angry with her for not being at the party this evening. She could have rung him up and bedazzled him again! We know Lance *went* to the Boundary Oak but we don't know if he is still there!"

"*Lance* is besotted with *Nimuë*?" asked Stinker, baffled and puzzled.

Finn decided he had to attempt to fill Stinker in on the facts even if it hurt him.

"I forgot you didn't know that! You have to stop composing all the time and get out more! Then you could keep up with the gossip, especially the bits that concern you. Nimuë is two timing you with Lance but also three timing both of you with Mordred. Mordred has been living in Little Wychwell for some time while pretending to be Phineas Floyd" said Finn.

Stinker sighed, "Do you think Mordred is still angry with me for going out with Nimuë at Oxford after the two of them broke up? Is that why he is attacking us? None of this makes sense to me! It is all getting a bit too much for me! Just when everything seemed to be going so well even though I was so tired! I might have known someone loving me for ever was too good to be true! Am I allowed to cry?"

"No" said Finn, "Not until we have got out of this crisis! We must exercise our mental efforts in hoping your very unfaithful very deceitful first love doesn't manage to kill us both and what we can best use to stop her. You can indulge in tears later!"

Finn was now standing edge on to the window, leaning against the wall so he could see but be out of range and sight from outside. Stinker crawled back and sat on the bottom step of the stairs, head in hands.

Stinker began to hum something.

"Why are you *humming*?" hissed Finn, "*Shhh*! I need to be able to hear what is happening outside!"

"Sorry, I didn't realise I was humming *out loud* but there was a good reason, assuming I get out of here I have just thought of some absolutely splendid opening phrases to a Requiem for Merlin! I am calming my disordered mind with composition you see" whispered Stinker, "I could write one for Arthur too, maybe some of the other knights as well, and have a set of Arthurian themed pieces! Arthurian themed requiems! Even commercial possibility there! They could sell well for funerals and memorials don't you think? As well as being amazingly beautiful and moving compositions I might even *earn* something! How about *this* as the opening for the *Merlin* Requiem?"

"*More requiems*! Don't you ever compose anything more *cheerful*?" asked Finn "Perhaps you should scribble a quick requiem for the two of us down just in case?"

"No manuscript paper or pen!" answered Stinker, now extremely jumpy again and looking round helplessly for either paper or writing materials that might have materialised by chance on the stairs, "Couldn't you, couldn't you just leave me to compose for a while in peace before I perish? Just so I feel happy *before* I die?"

Stinker looked at Finn and saw that Finn had a gun in his hand and a determined look on his face. But Finn also looked happy, confident and comfortable about his position, which is not what you really expect to see on your friend's face when he seems to be about to kill someone.

"I suppose *you* can't use a *gun* can you?" Finn asked Stinker.

"Funny thing, I very probably can, I used to belong to a Modern Triathlon club at Oxford, you know, before rowing expanded into all my spare time. There was shooting on the estate when I was younger too but I never cared for that at all, poor birds, too sad! I was a bit of a family disgrace when it came to shooting, I used to go and hide in my room!" replied Stinker.

"Splendid!" said Finn, passing him another handgun.

"I can *probably* shoot but there's no *point* in giving me this gun! I could not possibly fire at a *human*!" said Stinker.

"You'd be surprised what you can do in an emergency! *ducunt volentem fata, nolentem trahunt*[30]" said Finn, "Just make sure you don't shoot *me*! Or yourself. Fire at the robot if you feel too many scruples about humans! Might hit something vital or knock it over sideways, it's not very firm on its feet. *I'll* aim at the other two!"

A gigantic roar arose outside and approached the Wyching Well. An enormous vehicle headed up the road at its top speed.

---

[30] The fates lead the willing and drag the unwilling. Seneca

"Oh no!" whispered Stinker, "That sounds like one of the Boswell's huge tractors, she *has* called Lance back from the Boundary Oak to help her! That thing will ram straight through the front wall, Lance must know how easy it would be to ram through this wall and how to do it!"

The wolf was just lined up to start lumbering across the road so it could give what Mordred hoped would be a decisive blow on the door.

Finn was just about to suggest evacuation via the back door since they now knew Lance was at the front but before Finn could do so there was the sound of impact, followed by the sound of brakes being applied very hard. The bang from the impact was so big that all loose small items on and around the bar jumped into the air and then resettled themselves.

Finn had abandoned evacuation and thrown himself back on to the floor, dragging Stinker down with him. They waited for a few seconds. Nothing else happened.

"We are *dead men*!" quavered Stinker, who had his eyes tightly shut, "Why are we *still alive*? Is the tractor right inside the bar?"

"Don't be ridiculous!" said Finn, "Pull yourself together! The bang was *outside* in the street, obviously!"

Stinker opened one eye a crack, lifted his head and looked at the door, the hinges were still attached, the door was still there. He opened both eyes and sat up.

"What happened then?" Stinker asked.

"I don't know yet. Wait right there! It could be a *trick*" said Finn, sidling swiftly to the window and looking out edgeways again.

Just down the road from the Wyching Well there was a tractor skewed across the road. Nimuë and Mordred and the robot wolf were all high in the air on the tractor forklift arm. Nimuë and Mordred were slumped over from the force of the collision. Broken pieces of robowolf were strewn around the road.

Lancelot had ridden to the rescue on his tyred steed, rammed his biggest forklift tractor arm under the body of the wolf and then hoisted it into the air like a supersized bale of straw.

"*Lupus non timet canem latrantem*[31] or, in this case, of a speeding tractor... but it should have been!" pronounced Finn.

"No! No! No! Is Nimuë dead? Is she dead? Is she dead? If my love, my only love is dead how can I live now?" screamed Stinker. He began to wail on one high pitched note, on and on.

But Finn had already rushed out through the front door.

Lance climbed down from his cab and raised his hands above his head triumphantly.

"That's *fixed* her!" Lance yelled "That's *fixed* the little three-timing harlot! This village would have *tarred and feathered* them both in the old days!"

Lance then set off on some victory laps, waving his hands in the air and cheering himself, running round and round the tractor. Then he stopped running, threw his heavy jacket off and started doing saltos, backwards and forwards and then cartwheeled all the way round the tractor.

"I had no idea Lance was so good at gymnastics!" said Finn to himself.

Behind Finn there was the sound of Stinker still screaming in the bar, still on the same high note that went on and on and on. Finn ignored him.

After the cartwheels both Lance's white hot anger and his triumph cooled. Lance was now just a twenty three year old on his birthday who had been very stressed and distressed for hours and had a full stomach of alcohol too. Now he could not cope any longer.

Lance lay down on his face on the verge and started to sob "On my *birthday*, on my *birthday*! Not even *three* timing! There's *another* man on the wolf with her! Four *at least*! Whoever that is and Phineas and Stinker and me! All of us! The harlot! The bitch! The liar!"

---

[31] A wolf is not afraid of a barking dog.

Lance continued through a long list of rude names that he felt applied to Nimuë.

Finn decided to ignore him too and concentrate on keeping watch on the two who were slumped in the fork lift in case either of them recovered enough to make a run for it. Finn sat on a the wall outside the Wyching Well and hummed a tuneless little hum to himself. Things had not turned out too badly after all.

Who was coming now? There was the roar of a car engine approaching at full tilt and then a bright pink Vauxhall Astra with white daisies all over it hurtled up the road towards them at over seventy miles an hour and skidded to a halt just before it rammed into the skewed tractor. Mordred le Fake sprang out, gun in hand and surveyed the strange scene. Then he put the gun away again by stuffing it into the bosom of his dress again before either Stinker or Lance noticed it. Morgan minced over to Finn.

"My my! What *is* going on?" Flipper simpered loudly in Morgan le Fake's voice, "I feel all *fluttery*!"

"Late with the calvary *as usual*?" whispered Finn to Flipper.

"It's my *high heels*!" Flipper hissed back "Have you *tried* jumping out of a tree in a hurry in *high heels*? Or running in them? It's a wonder I didn't *permanently* damage both ankles!"

"Why are we whispering?" asked Finn, "Mordred and Nimuë are in another world right now, Stinker is still yelling so much he can't hear anything else and Lance is completely lost in his own misery!"

"Good point but if I talk any louder I shall have to be Morgan instead of me, just in case one of them hears, and her persona is so *exhausting*, darlink! I'd rather whisper" replied Flipper.

Flipper looked around again, slowly, noting all the details.

"I hate to say this, Finn old boy, but I only leave you on your own for *an hour* and you achieve *this*!" Flipper said.

Flipper waved his arm at the scene expansively. Lance sobbing on the verge, Stinker unstoppably hysterical, still screaming but now sitting on the threshold of the door to the Wyching Well, bits of robowolf scattered on the road, Lance's huge tractor slantwise across the road, Nimuë and Mordred and the rest of the robowolf all slumped pathetically in the tractor forklift, beer dripping down from the forklift, the main window of the Wyching Well badly damaged and beer still firing out across the pavement and road from holed barrels.

"It's *very* impressive!" Flipper continued, "*Definitely* one of your best messes *ever*! I could hardly have produced such carnage *myself*! What a good thing there is time to tidy up before anyone sees it because nearly the entire village is at the Pile On!"

"I made a mess! You *blew a house up*![32]" said Finn.

"You blew a much *bigger* house up![33]" retorted Flipper.

"No, I didn't! That was Mr Big, or rather Adam!" Finn responded.

"But it was *your* fault!" answered Flipper.

"No, it *wasn't*!" said Finn.

Flipper decided to change the subject before Finn remembered any more examples of carnage that he, Flipper, had achieved, as a few had just popped into his own mind.

"I say, the Wyching Well door held even though they kept ramming it with a huge robowolf!" Flipper said, "They knew how to make doors in the old days!" Flipper continued, admiringly, "Oak you know, stronger than almost anything! Good, strong, thick, solid oak!"

Then Flipper added, sotto voce, "Whole IT disabling project went as planned. Guess what! We were right. 100 small household generators for 100 servers in those cellars!"

"Plus two maniacs with a deadly robowolf as it turned out?" replied Finn, "No one thought to mention *that* little detail to me."

---

[32] All that Glisters is not Silver
[33] A Cellist in the Well

"No, no, Mordred must have kept the robowolf in the house he was using while he was Phineas Floyd, there was no robowolf in the cellars!" replied Flipper.

"So Nimuë and Mordred *did* come straight from Phineas Flynn's house!" said Finn, "That's good! It has only just occurred to me now that I already know they are safe that Mick and Ed might have been attacked by the robowolf first while the two of them were on their way to attack us!"

Finn did a quick calculation of small household style generator oil consumption translated into Kilowatt hours in his head and then continued, "The amount of oil that many generators would consume in a day explains why it had to be delivered so often. I suppose if Mordred had just plugged the servers in to the electric supply then the use would have shown up on the consumption figures for the household rather dramatically but he didn't realise the oil use from multiple delivery companies would also be noticeable. *Was* it a cryptocurrency exchange?"

"Mick and Ed haven't finished analysing what they have found yet" said Flipper "But that seems very likely. Bound to be a massive money-spinning scam or fraud or money laundering of some sort or even something that seems semi legal but with money only flowing in one direction to Mordred and then it can never be withdrawn again. You can make a packet on that sort of activity, until you get caught, so many people will swallow *anything* if tempted by a vision of immense wealth!"

Finn said "You had better tackle Lance and make sure he knows not to say *anything*, anything *at all*, before he nips back off to the Boundary Oak and tells everyone else! I am going take Stinker back inside the Wyching Well and keep handing him more and more double brandies till he either calms down or conks out!"

"No! I am *not* going to talk to Lance!" said Flipper, "Not doing anything of the sort!"

"Why not?" asked Finn.

"Because that would blow *both* our covers and I have instructions *not* to do that! Also I am going to compete in the Little Wychwell Clay Pigeon Shooting competition! Which I couldn't if my cover was blown now could

I? I can't let Alf down like that, the competition needs all the publicity it can get!"

"*What*?" asked Finn, "Have you lost your *brain*?"

"I am only here right now, fortuitous as it is, because Tristan was a bit concerned about the way Lance stormed out of the tree, Tristan having been telling him about Nimuë three timing him with both Stinker and Phineas Floyd. The entire village knew she was popping in and out of Phineas Floyd's house via the back garden it appears. I must have a word with Buffy about that, he forgot to mention that little detail to me. Possibly he was trying to spare Stinker from discovering that truth. So Tristan, after half an hour's consideration about what he had just told Lance became concerned that Lance might actually murder Nimuë. So Tristan asked me to follow Lance and make sure he was OK, as apparently no bona fide villager can leave a Pile On without an exceptionally good excuse. Otherwise I would still be up the tree and you would either need to commandeer a car or cycle to find a phone to use somewhere. Honestly I *just love this place now*! Perhaps I *will* retire and just live here for ever as Morgan le Fake!"

Finn sighed, "Well, that explains your sudden reappearance. I was thinking you must have received a psychic call for help from me! And you *can't* retire until I retire, I absolutely forbid it, where would I find anyone else quite so incompetent to work with who could make me look so much more efficient?"

"OK, OK, keep your hair on! I'll keep working! No, there were no secret Arthurian Vibes opening the psychic airways. I had *no idea* you were in danger. I was only worried about Lance getting life for murdering Nimuë. I must admit I wasn't at all worried about *her* being *murdered*. But you will be glad to hear that I transmitted a very quick non-psychic call for back up just before I got out of the Daisy Mobile" replied Flipper, "Mike and Ed should be along shortly, they were on their way back from rendering the servers non-functional so they when they turned round to come back they were already half way here. *They* can deal with debriefing Lance and Stinker and getting them to sign the Official Secrets Act or whatever" said Flipper.

There was a pause while Finn and Flipper both sat on the wall and enjoyed just not having to do anything much at all for a few minutes.

"So" Flipper then said, "What we *are* both going to do next is get Stinker and Lance back inside. We can stuff Stinker with double brandies if you like so he is passive and happy and fill Lance with black coffee to sober him up and then we will all just wait until further assistance arrives!"

But he was interrupted by cries from above, Nimuë had revived and was leaning over the edge of the forklift shouting at them, "Get me down! Get me down *at once!*"

"Get *yourself* down!" replied Finn, uncharitably.

"I can't! The stupid wolf has auto-locked the safety belts, they won't undo!" she replied.

"What a *shame!*" said Finn, "Don't worry, someone will be along to get you both out shortly and then arrest you for attempted murder!"

High pitched screams of rage and frustration joined Lance's loud and continuing stream of insults and Stinker's cries of woe.

"Lance has an astonishing vocabulary of insults don't you think?" Finn asked Flipper "What an impressive stream of invective. He's using several different languages too, that just proves there is benefit from a gap year abroad! I had forgotten there were so many other ways to say 'whore'."

"Try to get a quieter set of heroes and villains next time.!" said Flipper to Finn "It's a good thing Mordred still seems to be unconscious!"

"Should we check if Mordred is dead or dying or anything?" asked Finn.

"No" said Flipper, "Let's deal with rescuing the innocent General Public first. That is always the correct moral route. Even in our official training. We feel Mordred and Nimuë could be dangerous both to ourselves and the General Public so we must leave them where they are till reinforcements arrive. We cannot risk Stinker or Lance having apoplectic fits due to being in closer proximity to either of them! I'll see if Morgan le Fake can shut Nimuë up!"

Flipper changed voices and raised his voice so Nimuë could hear.

"Ooh lovey!" Morgan le Fake cooed up to Nimuë, "You'll have to stay there just for now! Don't want to risk climbing up there to get you down myself! I might get palpitations! Just you sit tight there, dearie, till a muscular Emergency crew come to cut you out! I *do* like a muscular Emergency Services man myself! You'll *love* being rescued, you know you will!"

"I *hate* you!" screeched Nimuë!

"Brilliant shutting up!" said Finn sarcastically.

"Give me a minute! I'm getting there!" said Flipper.

Finn laughed.

"Is Mordred *alive*, honeypot?" simpered Morgan le Fake.

"Yes, *of course he is*! I had brought some morphine with me in a syringe in case I needed to calm Mordred down, he was already right off the end with fury before we left. So I gave him a good injection of morphine in his shoulder just after I woke up to make sure he stayed quiet. He is going to be pretty wild about me and Lance if he ever finds out. I don't want to be stuck in a forklift with him having a tantrum. It's OK, he'll be out cold for *ages*! So you can count that as *me* rescuing *everyone else* from Mordred? That must be a 'get out of jail free' for cooperation card. *Now* will you get me down?" called Nimuë.

"No, dearie, just hold on in there for now, relying on you to stop Mordred falling out if the autolock wears off and the seatbelts unfasten, don't want a *murder* charge now *do you*?" purred Morgan le Fake.

Nimuë began to scream again in a manner very reminiscent of a steam engine whistle.

"Impressive!" said Flipper, "How long can she keep that up for do you think?"

"Judging by her previous vocal performances upstairs in the Wyching Well she could sustain that for hours at a stretch!" replied Finn.

Flipper turned to Finn, "And Lance and Stinker are this upset about finding she was three timing them? De gustibus non est disputandum[34] Hmmm!

It would be quieter inside and I need a cup of coffee myself! Do we have *biscuits* at all?"

"Bag of crisps do?" asked Finn.

"Done!" said Flipper.

"Or, at a push, I could do fried bacon and egg sandwiches?" suggested Finn.

"Even better!" said Flipper.

"For *four* do you think?" asked Finn.

"Definitely, it's vital for resuscitation of the innocent General Public and the stray passers-by, a.k.a. *me*, that we keep them nourished during the emergency. I myself have had a *terrible, terrible* shock and *need food!*" Morgan le Fake pouted.

Finn dug him in the ribs and went in, grabbing Stinker round the waist as he passed him and hauling Stinker behind him into the bar. Finn propped Stinker up in a chair, blew his nose for him, patted him on the shoulder, gave him a glass of brandy to hiccup and choke over and went to investigate what provisions he could rustle up.

Lance steam of abuse at Nimuë had finally ground to a half. Now he just seemed depressed in a sad and drunken way. Morgan le Fake teetered over to Lance, hauled him to his feet, persuaded him across the road and stuffed him into the bar. But then Morgan le Fake remained standing in the doorway, watching the forklift, one hand on the gun beneath his dress, waiting for Ed and Mike to turn up.

Stinker stayed slumped in the chair where Finn had put him, like a scarecrow without its supporting pole. Finn, Flipper and Lance left him there while they had a merry time with bacon sandwiches and coffee and then all sang Happy Birthday to Lance followed by the intake of a few slices of Mrs Boswell's wholly delicious cake, which even Lance was prepared to enjoy now that his acquaintances were not around to make fun of him having a cake with candles.

---

[34] No accounting for taste

A battered old green Ford Fiesta progressed at an unhurried speed down the road and parked outside the Wyching Well. Ed and Mike materialised from it and strolled casually over to Flipper.

"I see it's all under control now. Gather you've been on the tele!" said Ed to Flipper, "Powers that be are not enchanted!"

"It's OK!" retorted Flipper, "I'm a ghost! They can't sack ghosts!"

"No" said Ed "But they can sack Spooks!"

"Don't get over excited at the thought of my imminent departure from this job! I am *still employed*!" said Flipper "I had 'The Awkward Conversation' with them while I was leaning on this doorpost just now. They agreed that it was unfortunate that I had appeared quite so prominently on a news broadcast but that it had been *essential* for me to *remain in character*!"

"*So*" said Mike, surveying the scene, "what exactly *do* we have here? Did *you* make this mess Flips?"

"No" said Flipper, sounding superior, "Just for once it is nothing to do with me. Finn did this *all by himself*! It's a graphic illustration of what happens if you *auribus teneo lupum*[35]"

"Two persons stuck in a forklift, while still riding on a robowolf on which they are trapped due to automatically locked seat belts. That's what it says here on the job specification" said Ed "A bit of an uncommon scenario, I must admit. Just as well it's the *two of us* who got sent straight back, isn't it? I can see our really high-level IT ability and skills are *essential* here! Those who are not IT whizz kids might not have thought to use a 'high tech' box cutter to release them!"

Ed waved an industrial strength but completely mechanical box cutter at them as he spoke.

---

[35] Holding a wolf by the ears - a situation in which holding on and letting go could both be dangerous.

"I suppose we *have* to get them down now?" said Mike, "Such a waste of a trip to a charming country pub!" He called in through the door, "Pull us a pint while we are working, barman!"

"Not when you are *on duty*!" replied Finn, "I will supply you with lemonade if you wish!"

"Spoilsport!" said Mike.

An unmarked black car drew up beside the forklift.

"Ah, here's the rest of them! Best get going!" said Ed.

Ed and Mike lowered the forklift to the ground, released first Mordred, still in a drugged slumber, and then the apoplectically angry Nimuë. Mike and Ed dumped each of them unceremoniously into the back of the black car as soon as they were free. The car drew out and Nimuë and Mordred vanished from Little Wychwell.

Straight afterwards an unmarked white transit van pulled up. Two people wearing hazmat suits got out and the remains of the robowolf were removed from the forklift and the road, plastic wrapped and stowed in the van. Cleaning tools were produced, the road was cleared and everything from it was bagged carefully in plastic evidence bags.

"I hope none of that is dog shit or cow manure" Flipper whispered to Finn, who had joined him outside but now had to retreat back inside the Wyching Well for a few minutes to laugh.

One of the clearing team hopped into the tractor cab and parked the tractor correctly and neatly on the side of the road. Flipper was summoned to re-park his Daisy Mobile correctly.

Then the transit van drove off less than fifteen minutes after it had appeared.

A glazing van pulled up from the other direction and started work on the windows of the Wyching Well. It drove off half an hour later.

The Wyching Well and the road now looked as if it had been the usual, quiet Little Wychwell evening, except that the road was a little too clean.

Ed and Mike had debriefed first Lance and then Stinker.

Lance was *enchanted* to discover he had been part of something so exciting. His heartbreak over his brief infatuation with Nimuë was largely now assuaged by the pride and glory of *being a hero*, even if he was a hero who could never *say* that he *had* been one for the next twenty-five years.

After many warnings from Ed and Mike about not telling *anyone* else *anything* Lance was released and returned at once to the Boundary Oak where he announced, entirely untruthfully, to the contractors that his in calf heifer had given birth to a fine heifer calf and he was calling her Acorn in honour of the Pile On. He strode straight through their cordon back to the tree without missing a step.

"Did Nimuë *listen* to your viewpoint?" asked Tristan, anxiously, still guilty at not stopping Lance from dashing off and feeling that he must check that Nimuë had survived the encounter.

"You *could* say that!" said Lance, "She has *left the village*!"

"She is *alive*, isn't she?" asked Tristan, "She hasn't left this *world* as well as the village?"

"What do you take me for?" demanded Lance, "I wouldn't put a hand on a girl, well not in that way anyhow! We had a bit of a discussion but she accepted her promiscuous behaviour was unsuitable for a small village and has now returned to her parents' house!"

"Hooray!" said Tristan, while wondering exactly what Lance had said to Nimuë but also thinking that perching on the branch of a tree shouting at contractors was quite enough for one evening without having to listen to a post mortem on what Lance had been doing. Provided the girl was gone, that would do for him!

Back at the Wyching Well Stinker had listened very lethargically to Ed and Mike, signed where they told him to sign and then slumped face down on the floor of the bar and refused to move.

Ed and Mike vanished from the bar as though they were part of a disintegrating filter on Photoshop.

"Those two are *very* good!" said Flipper, "They fade out much better than we do!"

"Speak for *yourself*!" said Finn, "My disappearing without trace skills are *amazing*!"

"No, they aren't!" said Flipper.

"Yes, they are!" said Finn, demonstrating his ability in this field by calling this sentence down from upstairs.

"*Not* as good as Mike and Ed!" said Flipper.

"Yes I am!" said Finn, now speaking from behind the bar.

"*Not*!" said Flipper

"*Am*!" said Finn, ending his demonstration by being back next to Flipper for this comment.

"*Still* not as good as Mike and Ed! I *knew* you had moved each time!" said Flipper.

"At least I am not like a *thundering great elephant* trying to fade out by hiding behind a *tea leaf* like *some* people I know!" retorted Finn.

"No, I would say you are more like a *rhinoceros* lumbering around and trying to hide behind a buttercup!" said Flipper.

They glared at each other and then they smiled at each other and then they bumped fists.

They both considered the prone figure of Stinker on the floor.

"Well, *this* is a bit awkward!" Finn said to Flipper.

"Yes, we both have to hop it! Should already have left!" said Flipper, "But it's not really a problem! He won't have *any* customers tonight, they are all up an Oak tree, we can just lock up and leave him there!"

"Flipper!" exclaimed Finn, "We can't just leave Stinker there *on the floor*!"

"Why not? He'll get over it in a bit! Be fine by morning! Despair is usually a short-lived emotion! He won't hurt himself while he is lying flat on the floor!" said Flipper.

"You are *all feelings* sometimes aren't you?" said Finn, sarcastically. He considered possible options and added "Did you say *Buffy* is also *up the Boundary Oak*?"

"Yep, pretty much everyone from the entire village is either the Boundary Oak or else at the base of it unless they are minding the young or sick. Even *John* is in the crowd below the tree!" said Flipper.

"*Elodea*?" asked Finn.

"No, they left Elodea to look after Samaya, no children allowed at the Pile On! Health and Safety!" said Flipper.

"*Health and Safety*? In *this* village?" asked Finn "Well, thank goodness Elodea is still there! Come on, we'll have to drive him round to the Old Vicarage, you take his feet, I'll take the heavy end! Then you can drive off into the magic Arthurian Sunset in the Daisy Mobile and I can pedal away by bicycle!"

They lay Stinker across the back seat of the Daisy Mobile where he lolled uncommunicatively and then locked the Wyching Well up. Finn pinned a notice on the door saying 'Pile On At Boundary Oak' just in case anyone who had not heard this information should call in hoping for a pint.

Elodea was very difficult to startle or surprise after so many years of having children and grandchildren and the sight of Stinker being dragged into the kitchen by Finn did not ruffle her at all.

 Elodea was sitting reading a big picture book to Samaya who was on her lap. Samaya was pointing at the pictures in the book and laughing.

"Here! I've brought you *another* small charge to look after" said Finn, "He's a bit *upset*! Nimuë has gone back to her parents. *Good thing too*! But he is upset and I couldn't think who else to leave him with. I'm off now! Thank you for the loan of the studio and please thank John for me too. See you again in a few years I expect! Bye!"

Without waiting for Elodea to reply Finn dumped Stinker onto a chair and faded out through the door. Stinker collapsed in a formless pile, flopped over in the chair, head down towards the floor.

"Hi Stinker!" said Elodea to Stinker, "Lovely to see you, dear!"

Stinker groaned and did not lift his head.

Elodea propped Stinker back upright with one hand and then put Samaya in Stinker's lap and carefully wrapped his arms around her so she would not fall.

"Here! I need a break for a while! I am supposed to be making a gigantic cauldron of soup to take up to the Boundary Oak people and I am well behind time! *You* read to Samaya!" Elodea said, "She is holding her *favourite* book herself. We have only read it twenty times so there are at least another twenty times to go before she is *anywhere* near ready to go to sleep!"

Samaya was now making a noise that a siren business would have loved to record for later use and also kicking Stinker with both her feet while banging him on the head with her book.

But the effect of Samaya's attack worked. Stinker suddenly revived, sat upright, cuddled her in a firm grip, took the book from her hand, tapped her toes sharply with his finger and said 'No! Naughty!"

Samaya stopped screaming and kicking and looked at him with her mouth open.

Stinker jiggled Samaya up and down on his knee and sang her a nursery rhyme and she laughed and clapped.

Stinker smiled at Elodea, even if in a watery way, "I can look after Samaya for you! I can help! I'm *good* with small children!" he said, much to Elodea's surprise, who had only handed Samaya to him in the hope this might bring him back to the world, "I had *plenty* of practice with all my sisters!"

"You *have* sisters?" asked Elodea, who had somehow always perceived Stinker as an only child even though she knew his older brother had inherited the estate so he must have a brother.

"Ten of us altogether! Eight girls and my older brother and myself" said Stinker, "My Father always felt that was a *moderate* sized family as *he* was one of *fourteen*. We had nannies but even so I used to finish up having to look after the smaller ones at formal occasions and events sometimes."

Samaya reached out and tapped her book which was in Stinker's hand, "*Again!*" she commanded.

Stinker felt Samaya's soft warm body snuggling into his own. He hugged her to him and began to read.

"*No!*" said Samaya firmly, as Stinker tried to turn the first page over.

"You have to point to the pictures and name everything in them before you turn the page" said Elodea, apologetically.

Stinker started again. He named every object in the picture. Samaya smiled at him and gave him a big kiss on the cheek. Then *she* graciously turned the page over.

Elodea got back to chopping up an enormous pile of carrots and flinging them into the pot. She could see great future possibilities for babysitting by Stinker. Then she remembered that Stinker was usually at work in the evenings and sighed.

"Are you OK?" asked Stinker.

"Yes, I was just thinking what a good babysitter you would be if you were not working all the time!" said Elodea.

Stinker smiled, then a tear rose to his eye as he felt it was a long time since *anyone* had said he was good at *anything,* even composing, he *knew* he was good at composing but he never remembered good reviews, it was only the bad reviews that stuck in his mind. He had already forgotten that Finn had praised him for his defence strategy only that afternoon.

"The Wyching Well is closed on *Mondays!*" he said.

"You are *booked*!" said Elodea "Free dinner in exchange for an hour looking after Samaya! She was *such* an easy baby but the older she gets the more and more like a Smith she becomes, even if I shouldn't complain as I expect it is due to them having *my* genes, it can hardly be John's, he is *so* well behaved!"

"I would love that!" said Stinker, "Especially the dinner!"

Chapter Ten

Due to the Pile On the entire village had indeed been either up or just below the Boundary Oak or following the progress of those up the Boundary Oak on social media and local radio and TV. Thus the robowolf attack on the Wyching Well and the clearance operation were completely unobserved by anyone except the main participants and no one else has ever found out the real reason why Nimuë left so suddenly.

Tristan told everyone that Lance had been having a relationship with Nimuë and then discovered she was three-timing him and that he had told her she was no longer welcome in Little Wychwell in no uncertain terms.

A week later they realised Phineas Harper's had also left when, not having seen him at all for days, someone forced the front door to make sure he was not dead and found the house was clean and tidy and all his personal effects had gone as well as himself. As the Village said, "You couldn't really tell he was there when he *was* there, not exactly *social*!" It was later reported that he had taken a sudden decision to travel abroad for his health's sake although no one could remember who had started this rumour.

Phineas was then named by Tristan as one of the three timers, unlikely as this seemed. The Village decided that Phineas was frightened of Lance's superior muscle power. No one was concerned about the fact that Nimuë had left Stinker again. "Better off without her!" was the unanimous verdict in his case, "Stinker was much too good for a little liar like that! He'll get over it! Maybe we can all get some pints served *properly* and in an orderly fashion again without all those dreadful noises from above!"

Stinker even managed to come up with a reasonable explanation for Finn also disappearing.

"Author friend gone off to Hollywood again?" Robin and Jake asked Stinker.

"No, his girlfriend decided to forgive him and let him back into the house!" said Stinker, lying cheerfully, "She had thrown him out for coming in drunk once too often!" he added, happily denigrating Finn's character.

"Hope they have a big tree in their garden for him to sit up! He'll miss us all otherwise!" said Robin and chortled at his own joke, "Not that we haven't *all* been doing a bit of sitting up the Boundary Oak lately but that's different! That's for a *good reason*. Like sitting up one waiting to shoot deer. But some of your friends are just *a bit loopy* sometimes, aren't they?"

Not being able to say anything about the real facts has been stressful for both Stinker and Lance but if Lance comes into the bar at a quiet moment when no one else is there they are both able to reminisce and discuss the Day of the Robowolf. The Robowolf increases in size, strength and ability every time. Stinker and Lance are also able to discuss the dangers of falling prey to scheming and designing women and have made a pledge to *never* let the other *ever* do that again. They have devised a secret password to say very loudly to the other if they feel there is any danger of such an event happening.

Stinker was left with the many pages of manuscript that Nimuë had made him write. He kept it on is desk to start with so he could read it when desperate feelings of loneliness and desertion rolled over him. In the end he folded it all up carefully and locked it into a tin document case and pushed it under his bed out of sight. Then he took fresh clean sheets of manuscript paper and, with a sigh of relief at his freedom, began his own new masterpiece, Requiem for Merlin, "a brilliant and inspired piece combining pagan and Christian themes in one melded whole, deeply cathartic but ultimately hopeful" according to one of the many enthusiastic reviews that he received when it was complete. As a result of this fame the income that Stinker earned from royalties rose by several pounds per year.

The Boundary Oak was saved by the timely intervention of both villages. The contractors had to withdraw. The plans were changed. But, just in case of future danger, there is always someone from each village on permanent guard beneath it, day and night, ready to summon another Pile On if it is ever required.

***

A few weeks after the Robowolf incident Finn got a mysterious text containing a link to an Oxford Mail live feed article. Finn pressed the link.

'An Oxford Drag Queen has startled the other competitors by winning the Highest Award in the Little Wychwell Clay Pigeon Shooting Championships "I only learnt to shoot a few weeks ago so I am as surprised as everyone else!" said Morgan le Fake, "Alf is a brilliant teacher! I would recommend Clay Pigeon Shooting to anyone! So satisfying, honeypot!'

There was a colour photo of Morgan le Fake kissing a huge trophy.

Finn groaned "I am going to hear about *nothing* from Flip but his *absolutely amazing shooting* for *weeks* now" he sighed "Perhaps I will omit my early morning run for a few days till he has got over it? No! I had better get it over with tomorrow. I just hope he doesn't break the arm rest on that poor bench by doing handstands on it again[36]! The top shots in the Village must be *spitting blood*. Still Old Alf *will* be delighted! Such wonderful publicity for the competition!"

---

[36] Little Wychwell 9 Amare Valde

Chapter Eleven - Postscript

Barnabus was sitting on one of the red leather sofas in the Drawing Room with The Twin Emperors, Julius and Augustus. Barnabus was reading aloud to them as they poked at the pictures with their fat little fingers and laughed. Elodea brought in a tray with coffee, managed to get a cup to Barnabus without either of the twins tipping it all over him and then sat down on the other settee.

"I suppose the new sofas are not *so* bad" she mused aloud, "Cold, hard and uncomfortable but I must admit that they look quite good!"

"Also" added Barnabus, "much easier to wipe down after the twins spill things on them or have an accident on them!"

"Don't tell John you have been wiping them with water!" said Elodea, "He has a special spray and nothing else wet is allowed to contact the leather!"

"Some hope of *that*!" said Barnabus, "Must remember not to tell him about all the disasters that have already occurred!"

"*Read*!" said both the Twin Emperors together. "Read Lolhy! Lolhy!".

"I just *finished* it for the *third* time!" protested their Father, "Wouldn't you like a different book? Nonna has lots of lovely books right here!"

They both glared at him and shook their heads.

Barnabus sighed and re-opened the book. He was thankful that it was a picture book without too many words.

"*This is Ma*" he read, "*This is Lolhy. This is Puddles the Dog. This is Pa.*"

"Are you sure the two of you can't *remember* what this book says?" he asked, "I've read it to you often enough! You could turn the pages and say the words to yourselves?"

They both glared at him again. Barnabus sighed a deep and heartfelt sigh.

"Oh, go on!" said Elodea, "Just *read* it!"

"Have you read it?" asked Barnabus.

"No" said Elodea and added in an aggravating way, "So *I* would like to hear it *too!*"

The Twins smiled at her approvingly.

"OK" said Barnabus, "I'll read it and the three of you had better listen up and give it your full attention! Just don't say I didn't warn you about the dreadful experience you are about to have, Mama!"

"Lolhy had never had Head Lice. This was because Ma was the Queen of Head Lice Prevention. Ma mixed her own patent louse repellent mixture from herbs and oils and put it on Lolhy's hair every morning. Lolhy protested every morning that no one else in school smelt like that all day but Ma just yelled 'Prevention is better than cure! The only Good Head Louse is a Dead Head Louse!' and sprayed the louse repellent all over Lolhy's head.

Whenever Ma got a letter giving special warning about Head Lice at Lolhy's school then Ma screamed very loudly 'The only Good Head Louse is a Dead Head Louse!' Following the scream she put Lolhy and Puddles and Pa under a regime of combing and washing and oiling and careful scrutiny for the next week."

"Comb wash oil, wash oil comb, oil comb wash!" shouted both the Twins.

"An *unusual* book!" said Elodea, "Is Lolhy a girl or a boy?"

"It doesn't matter what gender Lolhy is" answered Barnabus, piously. "you are taking an ideologically unsound sexist attitude to gender which you might transmit to the Twins!"

"*What*?" asked Elodea and threw a cushion at him.

"Now you are encouraging the solution of disputes by using violence!" announced Barnabus and was hit by another cushion.

The Twins glared at Elodea, "No Nonna! Dad *read!*" they both said, "Nonna *quiet!*"

"Apologies!" she said to them, and to Barnabus, "Oh do get on with it!"

"But Lolhy secretly wanted to have Head Lice. Lolhy thought they would make Good Pets and how handy to have Pets you kept on your own head!" continued Barnabus, "But Lolhy never had a chance to have head lice because of the louse repellent. Other people in the class had Head Lice and Lolhy was jealous!"

"What?" shrieked Elodea, "I hope this book isn't an attempt to rehabilitate Head Lice!"

"I can't possibly give that away, it would ruin the plot!" said Barnabus.

The Twins glared at both of them, "Dad read! Nonna quiet!" they said again. Elodea glared at Barnabus. Barnabus continued.

"But then Ma had to go and visit Lolhy's Granny who was Ma's Ma. So Ma had to go away for a week. Lolhy saw a chance!" read Barnabus, "The following morning Pa tried to put Ma's patent lice repellent on to Lolhy before school. Lolhy screamed and shouted and said no one else in the class smelt like that. Pa said he did not suppose anyone in the class had head lice anyway. He asked if Lolhy had had a letter about any head lice yesterday? Lolhy said 'No!'...but Lolhy was lying for there was the letter hidden in a coat pocket. So Lolhy went to school with no head lice repellent on!"

"Hidden letter, letter hidden, hidden letter!" yelled both the Twins.

"Shhh!" said Barnabus, "I will continue! 'That day at school Lolhy looked around the class for someone who was scratching their head in precisely the way Ma had warned was a sure sign of having head lice! Lolhy stood right behind them in the lunch queue and Lolhy saw a Head Louse fall from their head right on to their jumper. Lolhy picked it up and popped it into a curl of hair! Lolhy was very happy and danced a little jig right there in the lunch queue!'"

"This is an awful book" Elodea complained, "It's rehabilitating head lice and encouraging bad behaviour!"

"I haven't finished it yet" retorted Barnabus "And if you don't stop interrupting I never will!"

Elodea gave him a fixed and angry stare at him. So did the Twins for the reverse reason and since the combined screaming of the Twins even outdid their Nonna when she was furious Barnabus hastily resumed his reading.

"So" continued Barnabus, "*Lolhy took the head louse home and was extremely pleased. Pa forgot about washing and combing hair that night or the following morning. By the end of the next day Lolhy was not quite so happy about this new pet which seemed to have turned into lots of new pets*[37]. *Lolhy's head had bites all over it. By the evening Lolhy was scratching her head furiously. Pa forgot about washing and combing hair again. The next morning Puddles had started scratching and by that evening Pa had started scratching too.*

'They haven't *got head lice in your class have they?' asked Pa.*

'No!' lied Lolhy who still had the letter about Head Lice hidden in a coat pocket. Ma would have checked through the coat pockets.

'Must be mosquitoes!' said Pa, "Or maybe ants?"

They all watched a football match on the TV and Pa completely forgot to comb or brush Lolhy's hair again that evening...or the following morning....and he forgot all about the lice repellent mixture too.

By the next evening the problem was much worse. Pa decided he had better comb Lolhy's hair out over the sink just in case it might be head lice. He was horrified. Lots of Head Lice were dropping off the comb into the sink, and then Pa checked his own and it was the same.

'This is terrible Lolhy' said Pa, 'We do have head lice. We are both going to be in the most awful trouble with Ma. But I don't know what to do about them. There is only one thing to do.'

Pa got out his mobile phone.

Two hours later Ma appeared. She had driven a long way in a hurry and was very, very angry

---

[37] This is quite correct, female head lice only have to mate once in maturity to carry on laying fertile eggs for the rest of their life so one head louse is enough.

Pa and Lolhy and Puddles looked at her face and quaked. Puddles and Lolhy tried to hide behind the settee.

'The Only Good Head louse is a Dead Head Louse!' screamed Ma, "All three of you, sit on that settee instead of trying to hide behind it and stay right there! Do not move an inch! I am going to have to scrub and clean the entire house shortly but I will deal with you three first!"

The three of them huddled together on the settee and trembled.

Ma went upstairs. When she came down she was wearing a full hazmat suit and had a huge box full of ointments and repellents and shampoos and conditioners and fearsome looking metal nit combs and plastic nit combs and electric nit combs.

'Where did you get all that lot from?" asked Pa, giggling nervously.

"I have had it ready for years!" yelled Ma, "Prevention is better than cure! The only Good Head Louse is a Dead Head Louse!"

Lolhy was not allowed back to school by Ma for a week.

For that entire week Lolhy was combed and washed and oiled... and washed and oiled and combed... and oiled and combed and washed for the whole week and so was Puddles.........and so was Pa. And then Ma started again on Lolhy. Round and round and round."

"Comb wash oil wash oil comb oil comb wash! Round round round!" chanted the Twins together, stabbing their fat little fingers at the pictures and then they both fell about laughing on the floor for a while.

"It's their *favourite* page!" said Barnabus to Elodea, then he said, much louder, "I will not continue unless you are both quiet and sitting down!" and both twins jumped back up on to his knees.

Barnabus read on, "But Lolhy did not mind all the washing and oiling and combing and felt happy that Ma was there to do it all because now Lolhy knew Ma was right...The Only Good Head Louse was .....a Dead Head Louse!"

The Twins had joined in with "The only good head louse is a dead head louse" with great enthusiasm and then they both rolled about the floor together again giggling hysterically.

"*THE END*" finished Barnabus.

The Twins ignored him, they were now having a play fight and punching each other.

"I suppose the *ending* is OK but that is one *weird book*. It comes of labelling so many books as ideologically unsound. You finish up being only left with something like that I suppose?" said Elodea.

"To be fair the pictures are *extremely funny* but you couldn't see them" said Barnabus.

The Twins stopped fighting.

"*Again*!" said the Twins, "Read again! *Nonna* read it!"

"*No, definitely not*!" said their Nonna in a voice that must be obeyed. She snatched the book from Barnabus and handed it to them both, "Here, you can look at the pictures and say the words *by yourselves*!"

"Does *Angel* like it?" Elodea asked Barnabus "It is a *terrible* portrayal of Mothers!"

Barnabus was thinking it was a rather accurate portrayal of both Elodea and Angel when they were cross, especially if you could see the pictures, but he kept that to himself. Out loud he said "Let's be fair, Pa doesn't come over very well either! No, Angel absolutely *hates* it, but maybe not entirely for the reasons you might think!"

"She hates it for other reasons than the offensive portrayal of Mother's as mad tyrants and lice as desirable pets?" asked Elodea.

"It doesn't really portray lice as desirable, it shows why you *should* avoid getting them, you didn't see the pictures of the bit where Lolhy and Dad and Puddles were suffering from them. Oh, and you had better be careful before being too rude about it as you know the author!" said Barnabus.

"I *do*, who is it?" demanded Elodea, "What a good job you warned me!"

"Dine S Wolfer" said Barnabus, waving the cover at her.

"I don't know *anyone* called that!" said Elodea.

"It's a very bad anagram" said Barnabus.

"Enid?" said Elodea, "First name must be Enid. But Wolfer? Wait a minute, I'll get it, who do I know called Enid? Oh no! It's not an anagram of Wolfer but of Swolfer! *Enid Flowers*! Angel's *Mother*?"

"Yes indeed!" answered Barnabus, "And it gets worse! Wait for this!"

Barnabus retrieved the book from Julius, who was thwacking Augustus with it, and handed it to Elodea open at the title page. Beneath the title it said '*Based on a true story about our own family*'.

"Guess who Lolhy is!" said Barnabus.

"*No!*" said Elodea, "I tend to forget Angel is really called Holly! Angel is Lolhy?"

"'Fraid so!" said Barnabus, "And Angel is *particularly* mad because she didn't think her Mother had ever found out that she had put a head louse into her hair *on purpose* at school."

"Mothers" said Elodea, "Know Everything!"

"Very true, Mama!" said Barnabus, "But in this case I'm afraid Angel discovered that her sister, who is not mentioned in the book but also suffered during the head lice outbreak, *betrayed* her. So now, even though this treachery happened many years ago, Angel and her sister are no longer speaking to each other. I am sure they will get over it shortly. Also Enid has not sold many copies of the *book* but she is selling a lot of her *patent lice repellent mixture* round their village, the parents love it! Apparently it *actually* works!"

"I suppose I have to tell Enid what a *wonderful* book it is next time I speak to her!" sighed Elodea.

"Definitely and absolutely!" said Barnabus, "She drew all the amazing illustrations for it herself you know! You could focus on those!" and then he continued to the Twins, "No, I'm *not* reading it again! Nonna doesn't want to listen to another story! Just play by yourselves! You must be able to think of something to play quietly that doesn't involve fighting or breaking things!"

So Barnabus and Elodea drank coffee and rediscussed the Boundary Oak and Stinker and Nimue and how school was going for all the children and what happened in church last week and many other bits of gossip. Meanwhile the Twins had decided to explore the darker corners of the new settees, pulling the big buttons on the back and lifting the cushions off so they could poke around under the edges of the seats.

"Ook!" said Augustus, waving an envelope in the air.

"Where did you find that?" asked Barnabus.

"Dere!" said Julius.

Barnabus took it from him.

Barnabus looked at the address on the outside. The envelope had been opened and the letter filed back in it.

"I say!" he said to Elodea, "Look at this! Could it have been in the sofa when Dad bought it? But it has this address on it!"

"I can't say *I* ever looked in the crevices" said Elodea, "I was too cross about the whole thing being bought and the room changed *without consulting me*! But I thought John did! In fact I am sure of it. Maybe the Twins shoved that letter is into the settee themselves when they were here before. It could have fallen out of one of the books when Dad tidied up. I *still* don't know why he did it! Without even *telling* me!"

"I think Dad wanted the new room to be a wonderful surprise for you after years of dust and decay, he was a bit *hurt* when you were angry you know!" said Barnabus.

"*Possibly!*" said Elodea and sniffed loudly, "You would think, after all these years, that he would have realised I would *not* be pleased! I am now *constantly* expecting to find he has tidied the kitchen next and ruined everything I like about my kitchen too! I shall finish up trying to make cakes with no baking tins!"

Barnabus, who had, in fact, helped John with his secret Drawing Room renovation, thought that removing all the tottering piles of old parish magazines and other unknown junk from the kitchen could only be an improvement. He and John had already agreed to tackle that project together on the next Bank Holiday. Barnabus tried to look very innocent and only got away with it because Elodea was untangling the Twins, Augustus had got a button tangled up in a buttonhole on Julius' dungarees.

Distraction, thought Barnabus! He must *distract* Elodea from the subject of the Kitchen at once! Fortunately Barnabus the letter he had in his hand might work!

"You should look at *this*. *Here*!" said Barnabus waving the letter at Elodea.

....to be continued in the next Little Wychwell book.

Printed in Great Britain
by Amazon

24622353R00096